IDA IN THE MIDDLE

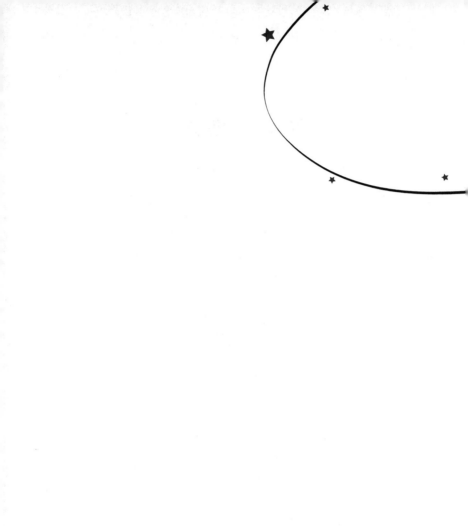

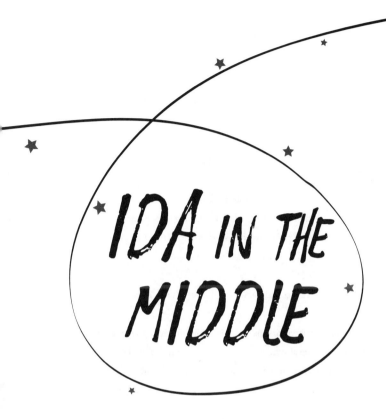

IDA IN THE MIDDLE

By Nora Lester Murad

Crocodile Books, USA

An imprint of Interlink Publishing Group, Inc.

www.interlinkbooks.com

First published in 2022 by

Crocodile Books
An imprint of Interlink Publishing Group, Inc.
46 Crosby Street, Northampton, MA 01060
www.interlinkbooks.com

Library of Congress Cataloging-in-Publication data available
ISBN-13: 978-1-62371-806-0

Printed and bound in Korea
10 9 8 7 6 5 4 3 2 1

For Kathie. For Navika.

Life continues.

Contents

I

1
Passion Project

As Ida scooted into her seat—third row from the front, second desk farthest from the door—her tennis shoe made an embarrassing, sharp squeak on the shiny linoleum, like the sound of sneakers on a gym floor. Ida gasped, then exhaled when nobody looked in her direction. She spread her notes over the desk and slumped down into the hard seat.

Ida had claimed this perfect spot at the beginning of eighth grade so she could remain unnoticeable, like the dust on last year's history books, and the spot had not failed her. The talkative kids all sat in the front two rows on the side near the door, which was to Ms. Bloom's left. Ms. Bloom, who most of the kids called Ms. Eva because she asked them to, must have had a chronically sore neck because she never looked toward the windows, and fortunately, the kids didn't seem to see Ida either.

From that invisible, anonymous spot, Ida could zone out when the class material was easy, which was always. She liked to look down onto the little footpath alongside the school building that nearly aligned with the border between her city of Oldbridge, Massachusetts, and neighboring Oldbridge Highlands. Ever since she could remember, edges and boundaries seemed to laugh at Ida, challenging her to a game of truth-or-dare. When her mind wandered too far, she imagined water trickling through the concrete pathway and seeping down into the soft ground where it belonged, and Ida felt herself coming back.

It was now more than eight months into the nine-month school year, and Ida was still the new kid at Riverview School. It had a reputation as a "special" K-12 school where kids were either a little too smart or a little too weird to thrive in the public schools, and their parents hoped an "innovative" program would bring out the Beethoven or the Meryl Streep or the Bill Gates in them. To Ida, the school wasn't special—it was strange.

The building was too new and felt like it was plopped down from the shelf of a toy store. The rooms were too colorful, and the fluorescent lights were so bright that the hallways made you dizzy, like the waiting room at the doctor's office. Even the temperature was controlled so that every day felt like the first day of second semester, when the end of school seemed a lifetime away. How could you know when it was time to be energized or time to slow down? When to want to go outside and when to be glad to stay in? What Ida hated the most was that the teachers were always happy—too happy. And even though they talked a lot about the "real world," it all seemed fake.

Ida was at Riverview because she had to be.

⋆⋆ ⋆

It was one thing in the fourth grade when the kids at Andrew Jackson Middle School started making fun of her name. They said she had an old-lady name, and the boys ordered her to knit them gloves and hats and slapped each other on the back laughing. Ida tried to explain that her name wasn't pronounced "I-duh." It started with an 'ayn, an Arabic letter that doesn't exist in English. She touched her neck to demonstrate how the sound starts way in the back of the throat, and how it kind of wavers like the "ah" sound you would make if you were falling off a ladder. All that did was whip up the other kids. After that, they waved their outstretched arms in circles and pretended to lose their balance whenever Ida walked by. She told them she didn't mind if they pronounced her name Ida as it would be in English, and it was true—she really didn't mind. But it didn't matter because by fifth grade, it was rare that anyone ever spoke to her at all.

Ida's father was furious at the way the kids treated her at Andrew Jackson. He pushed her to stick up for herself, because "you can't rely on anyone else in this world." But her mother told her to "rise above it." She figured that meant to shut up and get used to it. Every once in a while, a teacher would hear the kids and tell them to leave Ida alone. But the teachers called her "I-duh" too and didn't care about the 'ayn or about Arabic or who Ida was any more than the kids did.

But as Ida got older, the kids' harassment at Andrew Jackson got more sophisticated. In the sixth grade the school decided to "celebrate culture," and her classmates "discovered" that Ida was Palestinian, and somehow everyone knew, even though they were not likely told so, that being Palestinian was bad and not to be celebrated. Some of the religious Jewish kids started acting scared of her— even the ones whose birthday parties she'd attended every year since first grade! Everyone treated Ida as if she were a troublemaker just for existing, as if she should just stop being Palestinian so everyone else could feel comfortable. Or at least that's what it felt like. Whenever topics like abortion or the death penalty were discussed in class, the teachers would say, "We want to stay neutral about these kinds of controversial issues and not take a position"—and give Ida the side-eye.

Then, in seventh grade, things got much, much worse. There was an escalation of violence in Jerusalem that prompted some of the Jewish kids and a group of Christian kids to form a club called "Love the Holy Land"—and the school supported them.

"We give students a wide purview in their student-led clubs," the principal told Ida's father when he complained that the club was teaching kids a distorted perspective. "It's part of youth leadership and civic responsibility."

In the Love the Holy Land club, they talked about Israeli history and how Palestinians were trying to steal land that God had given to the Jews. They put posters all over the school inviting people to their book club and to hear speakers, most of whom were parents of the club members.

Desperate for help, Ida mustered the guts to talk to Principal Barrett herself when she ran into him in the hallway one day. Ida explained that she was being treated like some sort of dangerous outsider, and nobody would listen to her, or even just acknowledge that she was a person. Although she tried to speak clearly and use strong words like her father, her voice got small and wobbly as she held back the tears that came with anger.

Principal Barrett seemed to feel bad for Ida, so he suggested that she start her own club, a Muslim club. But there were only a few Muslims in school, and they were mostly Southeast Asian, not Arab. Ida's parents objected too, because not all Palestinians are Muslim and the problems in Palestine have nothing to do with religion. "What would a Muslim club do?" they asked.

Andrew Jackson Middle School had an anti-bullying policy, and so Ida's dad and mom wrote a letter to the superintendent of the district. But instead of telling the kids to stop bullying, he wrote back explaining that there are many different, legitimate views on just about everything. Part of Ida's education was learning to respect other ways of thinking, he said.

"Then why don't they respect our way of thinking?"

Ida remembered asking the other kids this question at the annual Palestinian picnic in a neighboring town.

It was supposed to be a break *from* school, but all the kids talked about *was* school. They had taken Ida's complaint as an invitation to share their own frustrations about being Palestinian at school.

> *"Nobody even says the word 'Palestine' in my school."*

> *"The teachers are afraid to teach about anything related to the Middle East—even if the topic has nothing to do with politics."*

> *"I was late starting school in the fall because we got stuck in Gaza during our summer visit. My parents went to talk with the school to explain and the dean of students launched into a lecture about antisemitism, as if Palestinians were responsible for the Holocaust or something."*

> *"My school fired a teacher for saying they support Palestine!"*

After a lot of discussion, Principal Barrett finally suggested that Ida's parents move her to a private school "for her own sake." When Ida's father explained that they couldn't possibly afford a private school, Principal Barrett found a way to get Ida a "diversity" scholarship to Riverview School, nearby. It was a private school, with a fun vibe and a good reputation for academics.

Ida was glad to get out of Andrew Jackson. But the way it happened made her feel like she was being swept into a trash bin after a messy art project. Now, at the end of her first year at Riverview, Ida just wanted to lay low and stay under the radar until she was old enough to move away, wherever "away" was.

⋆ ⋆*

"Guess what? Guess what?"

Ms. Bloom interrupted Ida's daydream.

Ida's teacher was sitting in the lotus position on top of her desk, wearing socks and sandals (she really was the only adult Ida had ever seen pull off that look). Ms. Bloom said that yoga kept her young, and she would sometimes cha cha cha around the room. Sometimes she even made the kids do stretching exercises at their desks, which was really embarrassing, but it fit in with the whole make-the-world-a-better-place theme of her class.

A boy stood up and made his voice sound like a little girl, as if he were doing a comic sketch.

"School is cancelled for the rest of today?"

His jeans were so far below his butt crack, Ida had to look away.

Unlike in Mr. Collins' homeroom class for the technology track or in Miss Takaki's homeroom for the business track, there was lots of joking and laughing in the social justice track.

"You wish," Ms. Bloom shot back. "I'll give you a hint. You know your Passion Project?"

Ms. Bloom had talked the class's ears off about the passion project practically every day for two months, and every time she did, Ida wanted to melt into nothingness, trickle down the footpath outside, and soak into the moss just like the water she so often imagined. Thanks to last week's science lesson, Ida knew that pretty high temperatures were needed to turn herself into a liquid, so instead, she dutifully turned to the page in her notebook that said, "What are you passionate about?" Underneath she had copied the instructions from the whiteboard: *Explore something important to you. Show the meaning it has in your life. Choose something you are proud of.*

The passion project was the eighth-grade "capstone" for the entire region. It had something to do with the student-led civics project that got added to the standard curriculum. Ida knew it was important but had treated it like her older sister, Danya, said to treat a zit: don't touch it and it will eventually go away (not that Danya followed her own advice). If Ida could translate her anxiety about this project into jet fuel, she'd surely have enough for a couple of trips to the moon.

"...So instead of submitting your work in writing," Ms. Bloom announced enthusiastically, "you get to make a presentation to the whole school community! Two weeks from today!"

The word "presentation" catapulted Ida's stomach into her throat.

"And there's more..."

Ms. Bloom spoke louder to drown out the whispers and stomping and rustling of kids looking around at one another trying to decide what to think.

"Focus up here people!"

She snapped her fingers over her head.

"On Saturday, before the school-wide presentations, five kids from our school will represent Riverview at a regional competition to see which eighth graders, and which schools, show the most passion!"

"But isn't that the night of our choir performance?"

Sean was a soloist in the choir. He was so tall, his voice rang out past everyone else's, even when he sang harmony. He could hold a note so long it sounded like a car horn.

"Postponed. But don't worry. We'll fit that in before the last day of school."

"But why, Ms. Eva?"

Sean sounded crushed.

"Because a TV crew wants to film the best presentations!"

Ida nearly sunk right through her chair into the floor. She reached unconsciously for the pendant around her neck and rubbed a finger back and forth over the raised Arabic engraving while she tried to catch her breath.

"We get to be on TV?" someone blurted out.

"Only five kids from each school will be chosen to present at the competition, but you'll all be considered."

There was about a half second of silence as the news sunk in, and then the class went wild. It took Ms. Bloom a whole five minutes to calm them down so she could talk.

"The studio will film the competition and use some

of the clips in a documentary about innovative teaching methods."

There were gasps and whispers as the students shifted in their seats. Ida watched, too shocked to move, as several hands shot up.

"Janey?"

As usual, Ms. Bloom always called on Janey first. Janey's mother was from India, and Janey's complexion was almost the same as what Ida's family called Ida's "summer color." Like Ida, she always got top grades. But Janey was popular, and her father was on the school's Board of Directors, so they lived in different worlds.

"Are we supposed to read our papers, or can I change mine into a PowerPoint?"

Ida glared at Janey who was sitting right in the middle of the front row. *She already wrote her paper?* Ida fumed.

"You can read your paper or show a PowerPoint, perform a poem or make a short movie—whatever you want. But I encourage you to be creative, because whether or not you end up in the competition, your passion project is an important part of your grade for the year, and the impression you make in your presentation will position you for success in high school."

Ida felt the walls close in on her, walls with eyes that could see right through her and into her fears. When she glanced around the room, her eyes locked with a girl named Lizzie, who seemed to be half-smiling at her. A smile that seemed to say the game was over—Ida had been found out.

When the bell rang marking the end of homeroom period, Ida scooped her papers and notebooks into her backpack. A wave of panic at the thought of her passion project assignment made her grab hold of the desk to steady herself, and as she stared down at the desktop, layered with doodles and emojis, she felt a rock the size of Plymouth land right on her chest. Hidden among all the scribbling on the imitation wood, nine letters in green marker came into focus.

T-E-R-R-O-R-I-S-T.

2
Killing Trees

Less than two weeks before the presentation, Ida hadn't written a single word. She might as well have tattooed "keep walking, no passion here" onto her forehead. She had lost all hope of getting an A. In fact, she was sure she was going to fail her assignment altogether and look like a fool in front of everybody.

But how could she even think?

Throughout the school day, her eyes darted back and forth across the rows of seats, over the round tables in the cafeteria, and through the hallways, trying to figure out who had written that ugly word on her desk. Was it that girl, Lizzie? Or were all the kids in on it? They seemed to be ignoring her as usual, but she couldn't shake the feeling that she was wearing a target. That at any second, someone might tell lies about her to her teachers, yell at her, or attack her or something. Ida had seen pictures and heard stories of terrible things being done to Arabs and Muslims after 9/11. She couldn't get the images out of her head of the Sikhs whose turbans were ripped off and the Arabic signs on stores that were spray painted.

Could Ida handle any of those things, if they ever did happen? Or would she give in again and run off to a different school, biding her time till the next incident, when she'd run away again?

With a totally unproductive day at school behind her, Ida was glad to go home.

Instead of going up to her apartment, she walked behind the building to the plot of dirt adjoining the parking lot. It had been designed for decorative shrubbery, but even the hardiest variety was thwarted by the shade of the building's upper floors. Swords of green-brown weeds mixed in with curly leaves and yellow clover flowers, making the plot an attractive place to play.

On Tuesdays, Ida's father coached a little-kids soccer team on that unlikely spot. He had started when Ida's big sister, Danya, was four, and he kept on doing it, even when it was Ida's turn to join the team and she refused because, as Ida put it, it wasn't right for the players to kick a defenseless ball. Now even her younger sister, Salwa, had "graduated" from the team. But Dad kept coaching.

It was kind of a family tradition to meet at the field after school on Tuesdays during soccer season to cheer the little kids on. Ida smiled when the ball, even if accidentally, reached the tree stumps that marked the field's edge and her dad called out a heartfelt "Goooooooal!" in his thick Arabic accent, his arm shooting high into the air in a victory gesture. On the soccer field, Ida's father was joyful, as if he was still a kid playing in the Palestinian village he'd left almost twenty years earlier. *Is that passion?* Ida asked herself.

The whole family knew that what Ayman did wasn't really coaching. The four-year olds were still working on basic concepts like sharing, and once they'd been convinced to share the ball, they had to learn not to share it with their friends on the opposing team.

Nearly all the children had immigrant parents, some undocumented. They looked like a little United Nations as kids of all colors and shapes ran up and down the field—or sometimes sat right down in the middle of it. Several languages were spoken, but few of the kids could speak much English.

Although Ida didn't like gross and whiny little kids, she felt some sympathy for them. She could relate to the doubt, fear, and confusion they would probably feel as they grew up in a place that talked a lot about fairness but gave weapons to bad people in their home countries, and then pretended they were the good guys. Ida wasn't the type to watch the news or read the Sunday newspaper, like her parents. But she knew that these kids were growing up with the same confusion that she felt, and that some of them might even be accused of being terrorists, just because of the way they looked.

"Ida!" her father called from the field. "Come over here and show Emmet how to keep track of where the ball is."

Ida was standing next to Danya, who was sitting under a mature sugar maple trying to memorize a poem for her tenth-grade poetry club.

"Would you go, Danya, please?" Ida blurted out.

Feeling safe under the shadow of the tree, she had been deep in thought about escape. There was so much to escape from, and no one to confide in about how she felt.

"Dad called you, not me."

"I don't know anything about soccer, and little kids don't like me," Ida said, moving backward into the dense leaves of a low branch.

"You're an idiot," Danya said, putting down her book and sprinting onto the makeshift field.

Danya put her arm around Emmet's shoulders and pointed to the ball and the two goals.

But Ida's mother called out, "Snack time!" interrupting everything.

She and Salwa had cut green and red apples into eighths and put them in a large plastic bowl with toothpicks so the kids wouldn't touch the food with their filthy little-kid hands.

"Now, Somaya?"

Dad shot Mom a look like she'd stopped the World Cup or something.

Mom just smiled and shook her head, without even looking up from the food.

On the way to get apples, a girl named Ayana tripped on a sprinkler and fell face down in the dirt. Without thinking, Ida ran to her before the other kids noticed. She brushed the light brown dirt off the girl's dark brown skin. Tears were brewing, so Ida pulled a Tootsie Roll Pop from her jacket pocket and whispered in the girl's ear.

"Keep this for later so no one else sees. I only have one, and it's for you, Ayana."

The little girl broke into a huge grin and bounded toward the apples with their secret in the back pocket of her jeans. Ida was relieved that no one saw what had happened.

⋆⁺ ⁺⋆

Later, Ida's family sat around a late dinner and, following routine, Mom asked each girl about her homework.

"I'm supposed to eat something healthy and tell the teacher about it tomorrow," Salwa said, reaching for the bowl of *lubya* to scoop onto her rice.

The juicy green beans were smothered in spiced tomato sauce and sprinkled with diced lamb.

"That's convenient," Dad smiled at Mom, as he poured her a glass of water.

"Third grade sure is yummy, isn't it?"

Mom touched Salwa's cheek.

"What about you, Danya?" Dad followed up.

"Finished."

Danya didn't elaborate, and Dad didn't make her.

Ida quickly shoved a huge spoonful of *lubya* into her mouth, hoping her parents would overlook her, but she wasn't so lucky. As they stared at her expectedly, Ida wanted to tell her parents about the mean thing written on her desk, about not having any passion, about wanting to escape from the haters. But they could never understand how it feels not to belong anywhere, could they? Her mouth too full to speak, Ida looked desperately at Danya, and Salwa, wishing they would come to her rescue. But her sisters couldn't see the knots in Ida's stomach. They kept eating and her parents thought Ida's silence meant that, like her sisters, she was finished with the day's tasks.

✦ ✧

Long after she'd gone to bed, guilt and fear plagued Ida. If she made a fool of herself at the passion project presentation, her whole family would be ashamed. But even if she thought of something to say, some mean person in the audience might still shout out an insult, and that would shame her family, too. Ida pulled out the pen with the little flashlight on it that she kept under her bed and tried to write some ideas for the passion project without waking her sisters. She tried hard. But all she ended up with were pages and pages of nearly blank paper scrunched up in the trash can and a guilty conscience for needlessly killing trees.

3
Home Bound

Ida always had butterflies in her stomach on Wednesdays, like she was waiting to get her report card. Dad had an afternoon practice at school, and Mom had the late shift at the radio station where she worked as a receptionist. Danya went to ballet class straight from school, and Salwa went to a friend's house until Mom picked her up. So, when Ida got home, after school, she braced herself. Nobody would be there: no Mom to envelop her in a hug that smelled cool and slightly bitter like fresh sage. Most kids her age craved time away from their parents—but not Ida. Arriving home alone that day, she felt a sense of dread heavier than her overstuffed backpack.

At the glass security door that led to the lobby of her building, Ida reached up for the buzzer, before turning toward the security camera to wave. In all her fourteen years of living in the building, she had never seen anyone be denied entry. Sometimes she wondered if Fernando and Alberto, the guards, were really in the little room watching on the screen, or if the buzzer was just set to let everybody in.

The elevator didn't work without a key. Ida pulled the piece of soft yellow yarn that hung around her neck out from under her t-shirt. She checked to be sure the pendant was still there—a small, plain, silver rectangle engraved with *Ayat al-Kursi* from the *Quran*.

Although no one in her family was especially religious, Ida's Aunt Malayka had sent the pendant to her, perhaps to make up for the fact they'd never met. The pendant sat in Ida's jewelry box for years. But when her aunt died recently, Ida felt she should add it to the necklace on which she wore her keys. It made her feel like someone was watching over her.

Ida inserted the smallest of three keys into the elevator lock. She pushed the button for the ninth floor and leaned back against the mirrored wall so she wouldn't have to look at herself. Ida was resigned to her "exotic" appearance. For the most part, she considered it a blessing that she could pass as anything. When she visited her best friend, Carolina, in her parents' restaurant, she passed for Salvadoran. When she went to the city to pick Danya up at ballet class, she passed for Greek or Italian. The only time Ida couldn't pass was when her parents spoke to her in Arabic in public.

Ida and her sisters understood Arabic, but they always chose to answer in English. That didn't protect them from the wide-eyed stares they often got when strangers heard the word *"Allah,"* which was mixed into many common Arabic expressions. At those times, Ida felt embarrassed. Then she felt ashamed that she felt embarrassed; then she felt guilty that she felt ashamed. And even though her parents and sisters all had the same experience, they kind of pretended like it wasn't so.

As usual, the elevator stopped on the third floor for no reason. When the door opened, the yummy smells of cumin and coriander revealed that her Pakistani neighbors were home. The door closed after what felt like an eternity (Ida had to go to the bathroom), and the elevator continued on. Then, for no reason, it stopped at the fourth floor, and the yummy smells of lemongrass and ginger disclosed that Ida's Vietnamese neighbors were home. It didn't stop again until it reached the ninth floor, where Ida walked out into the empty hall.

Most of the apartments in her building had turned over many times since Ida was born, as some families went back to their countries or got a good enough job to move to a better place. Ida's family had become the go-to for new families who needed to ask questions about how to catch the bus or what to do about moth infestations. That day, not too many people seemed to be home on Ida's floor, or if they were home, they weren't cooking. The hall just smelled stale.

Ida used the big key on her yarn necklace to get into the apartment. She put her grimy outdoor shoes on the mat to the left of the door and slipped into her fuzzy, purple cloth house slippers. She turned to lock the double bolt and gave herself a mental pat on the back. She usually forgot to lock the double bolt, and she usually got in trouble for it. Mom and Dad didn't seem to understand that remembering stuff like that was as difficult for Ida as math was for Carolina.

Ida tried to remember to make her bed, to put her clothes away, to clean her dishes from the table. She tried hard. But her mind always wandered off, never settling on any one thing long enough to follow through. In the bathroom, she was careful not to kick the rug into the corner, but she didn't notice that the towel wasn't securely on the bar after she dried her hands. It fell into a damp pile on the floor. Today, Ida noticed, concentrating was especially hard. Should she think about feeling lonely? About feeling scared of her passion project? Or should she admit to the deep helplessness she felt knowing that people in her school, not to mention in the rest of the world, thought that she and her family were evil?

Ida drifted to the big living room window to look down on the Oldbridge traffic. Although she knew the window didn't open, she touched the pane gently, just enough to reassure herself that she was inside, home, safe. *Those people have passion*, she thought to herself as she tried to imagine the people in their cars. *They probably get up early on the weekends and take food to homeless people. Or maybe they write hit songs and donate the money they get. What am I going to say in my presentation, when I don't even do anything?*

The plastic gimp that Ida used to make friendship bracelets was sitting on the coffee table, although Mom had told her about a thousand times to put it away in the art drawer. Ida tied a couple of knots before she lost interest and put it back on the coffee table. She picked up the guitar her father bought her at a garage sale after she had begged for it. But hearing the screechy metal sound she made with it just made her feel even more untalented and clumsy.

Ida plopped down on the couch, sending Mom's gazillion embroidered pillows flying. Some were covered with the bodices of traditional Palestinian dresses that Mom had bought in the Old City of Jerusalem. When the dresses wore thin, they would cut out the neck and chest sections and reuse them for decoration. Ida picked up a pillow and marveled at the tiny and nearly perfect red and white cross-stitch. She traced her finger over the orange, green, and black fishbone stitch on another. It must have taken hours and hours of patient attention to embroider even one dress, much less a wardrobe. *Is that what passion is?* Ida wondered.

Ida decided to focus on the homework assignments that were due tomorrow. For personal financial literacy, she had to calculate the cost and price of different kinds of cookies by volume and weight, while keeping the profit margin constant. Plus, she had to do some writing about the role of cookies in her family economy. Then there were two long and boring chapters about migration.

She picked up the world geography textbook, which seemed to weigh about a hundred pounds. She started reading about how people moved all around the world, especially in the 1940s and 1950s. As she read, she highlighted dates in yellow, people's names in pink, and places in green, and then made a list in her notebook of all the facts that might be on the test. She smiled as she imagined her mother looking over her shoulder saying, "Is it really possible that not a single woman did anything worth mentioning in your book?"

Done.

It took over an hour, but she was glad to have something to keep her mind off the passion project. Next was math, which was easy as usual, and when that was done she had nothing to do except to think about her passion, or lack of it.

Danya wanted to be a ballet star or, if that didn't work out, a teacher. Salwa loved science. Carolina wanted to be a photographer and already had a portfolio!

Ida's anxiety started to bubble over, like the time she left Mom's lentil soup on the stove with the flame turned up high. In desperation, she reached for the house phone. Ida didn't have a cell phone. Her parents said that cell phones and social media were the reason why teenagers in the United States were so ignorant about the rest of the world. Her parents blamed everything—rudeness, laziness, sex before marriage, even teen suicide—on cell phones and social media. Even Danya, who was older and really needed a cell phone to get around Oldbridge, had given up trying to convince their parents to let her have one.

But secretly, Ida agreed with her parents. She didn't want to be one of those kids who sat on the bus looking at a screen, walked around school looking at a screen, and went to parties looking at a screen.

"Hi, Mrs. Duarte. I'm sorry to bother you. Could I please speak with Carolina?" she asked sweetly.

Ida had a reputation for having the best phone manners.

Even her Dad realized she deserved credit last year after a boy in her study group at Andrew Jackson called the house, said "um" about ten times, forgot who he was calling, and hung up.

"Hey!"

Carolina came on after a minute, clearly glad to be distracted from her own boredom.

"Hey. Finish your homework?" Ida asked, settling into her normal after-school chitchat with Carolina.

"I guess so. I mean, I read the chapters, but it's only been ten minutes and I've already forgotten them," Carolina admitted.

"My mom says I have a short-term memory problem too," Ida said to make her feel better.

"History is just so boring!" Carolina complained. "Who cares what happened like two million years ago?"

"Human beings weren't even on earth two million years ago," Ida corrected.

"Don't be a jerk. You know what I mean."

"Yeah, I do."

Ida twirled the coiled cord of the phone over her pinky.

"How's your passion project coming along?" Carolina asked gently.

Carolina had to do a passion project at Andrew Jackson too, and she was excited.

"Not everyone is like you, ready to jump up and tell the world about yourself," Ida snapped, then regretted saying.

"No one wakes up ready, Ida. You have to *get* ready. And you're not going to get ready if you keep *procrastinating!*"

"I'm not procrastinating!" Ida said defensively. "I'm busy with other things."

"Really? I bet you finished math, didn't you," Carolina said, half-resentful and half-impressed.

"It wasn't that hard! Want me to help you with yours?"

"No. Mama says I have to do math myself. She says I'll never be allowed to close the cash register at the restaurant if I don't figure out how to do math."

Ida took the opportunity to change the subject.

"You're so lucky."

"Lucky? Lucky?"

Carolina liked to act shocked all the time.

"Yeah. You get to work at a real restaurant. And you even get to earn money."

"Well I think you're the one who's lucky."

"Why?" Ida snorted by accident.

"Because your hair and clothes don't smell like grease all the time."

"Well, that's true." Ida wasn't sure what else to say. "But, I have other, um, complications."

Ida knew Carolina would support her, no matter what. But she'd been hoping that if she pretended nothing was wrong, she could fade back into invisibility in her new school. It was so hard to say out loud how it felt to be misunderstood.

"Okay, I'll bite," Carolina said.

"Well," Ida sighed. "It seems the kids at my new school found out that I'm Palestinian."

"You *are* Palestinian, Ida! What's wrong with that?"

"But it's happening all over again. They think I'm a terrorist. They don't know me, but they hate me."

Ida was surprised how big of a relief it was to tell someone what was going on.

"Shit!" Carolina reacted. "Oh sorry, I know you hate cursing."

"It's okay. That's probably the right word to describe it."

"Are you going to tell the principal?" Carolina asked.

"My new principal won't care anymore than Mr. Barrett did. Neither will the teachers. They think I'm controversial just because I exist."

"I wish I could say you were wrong," Carolina responded.

"I know."

"What did your parents say?"

"I didn't tell them," Ida admitted. "My dad is still upset about this whole school thing. Mom says he was angry at Andrew Jackson for forcing me out. But I think he was disappointed in me, too, that I didn't stick up for myself well enough. And then when Principal Barrett got me that scholarship, my dad got even more upset. He's happy that I'm going to a private school that he could never afford. But Mom says he's ashamed that I'm in a school where we really don't belong, because they forced me out of the public school where I really do have a right to be."

"My dad was upset when you left Andrew Jackson, too," Carolina admitted. "I mean, my whole family loves you and wants the best for you. But it didn't seem fair that you got the scholarship and no one else did. But everyone could see that the way they got rid of you to make it easy for themselves was really fu… I mean, really messed up. Like *really*."

Ida remembered the night when the family decided that she should take the scholarship—despite the humiliation—and move to Riverview School. Her dad had leaned back in his chair and looked at the ceiling for a long time, not talking. The green-blue veins on his temples were throbbing, and her mom kept her hand on his knee as if to steady him until he finally broke the silence and told her to change schools.

"I just don't want to worry my parents by telling them that it's happening again," Ida agonized.

"But they love you, Ida."

"I know."

"And *I* love you," Carolina offered.

"I know," Ida exhaled and suddenly felt so exhausted that she could've slept for a year.

She was grateful that she could count on Carolina not to make a stupid joke like, "I love you even though you're a terrorist." Most people just didn't get it.

"Well, I'd better go," Carolina said after a long silence.

Ida put down the phone. But she immediately felt trapped, again. She groaned loudly, pulled a sheet of paper out of the recycling drawer and wrote "My Passion" at the top. After a few seconds, she drew a tic-tac-toe board and lost a game against herself.

4
Escape?

By five o'clock, her stomach was rumbling for real. Mom always joked about Ida's appetite. She was known to get hungry not only between meals, but between snacks, too. Mom usually gave her healthy "treats," as Mom called them, like carrots and chickpea *hummos* or a *za'atar* sandwich with spicy thyme and sesame seeds, which Ida absolutely loved. But she was giddy to have the freedom to eat whatever she wanted. It was the only good part of being home alone on Wednesdays.

Ida stepped into the tiny kitchen, barely big enough for two people. After all these years, Mom still complained about the kitchen. How could she possibly make good Palestinian food without enough counter space for chopping cucumbers and tomatoes for Arabic salad, much less for stuffing peppers with ground meat and rice? And the refrigerator wasn't big enough. "At home," Mom would say, "we had a refrigerator twice this size and a full-size freezer." This usually caused Dad to throw up his hands with an ambiguous expression that could have meant, "I am so sorry I dragged you here" or "It's your fault that we came here" or "What do you want me to do now, we're here!" Ida never followed up to find out which it was.

Mom was a good cook. But no matter how much food she stored in the little kitchen, Ida could rarely find anything to eat, and today was no different. She stood in front of the open refrigerator for a long time, staring blankly. She stood there so long she even forgot what she was doing, until her stomach reminded her that she wanted a snack that would hold her until Mom got home and made a real, hot meal.

Ida opened the upper cupboards to the left of the sink and found extra bags of rice and sugar, each double wrapped in a plastic bag to discourage ants. Mom kept the kitchen spotless, and there were rarely ants. But in the summertime, they seemed to congregate in summer camps just like humans, and the ant campers set out on field trips (wearing their camp T-shirts, Ida imagined) in search of crumbs. One summer, Ida and her sisters left their empty cake plates on the table and went down to the parking lot to ride bikes. When they got back, there was a parade of ants from a small hole in the wall. The girls refused to eat on the table for days after the ants were cleaned up. Dad was furious, not about the ants, but about the girls' reactions. "Don't you know that Palestinian women are farmers? How

can you be Palestinian and be scared of some tiny bugs?"
His "lost-my-temper" voice had thundered through their
apartment, letting the neighbors into their private world.

In the lower cupboards to the left, Ida found cereal.
But she knew that Mom monitored the level in the boxes
and would know if she indulged. Fruit Loops and Captain
Crunch were strictly for dessert, and only once or twice
a week. Unlike the ban on cell phones and social media,
this was not a rule that Ida agreed with. *Maybe just a little?*
She opened each cereal box and stuffed a handful into her
mouth. Then, she rolled the plastic liners down evenly the
way Mom did and returned the boxes to the cupboard just
as they had been.

Deep inside, Ida knew she had to work on her passion
project presentation. Standing in front of all those people
with nothing to say would be even worse than standing in
front of them and saying something stupid. Besides, she
would fail the assignment, and maybe the whole year, and
her parents would be disappointed, and she'd never be able
to show her face at school again, and she'd be arrested for
truancy, and her parents would lose their jobs trying to save
her, and they'd have no money and have to live in a shelter,
and her sisters would get sick from the drafty windows and
die, and her parents would blame her and abandon her in
the night, and... Ida's mind took off. But it would be even
worse if she went up there and someone shouted "terrorist"
and her father stood up to defend her, and then everyone
would attack Dad, and Mom would jump in front of the
attackers and there'd be a fight and her parents would get

killed and her sisters would blame Ida and she'd be an orphan...

Ida went to her bedroom and took out a sheet of paper. She scribbled words on it like her English teacher taught her to do when she was brainstorming topics for an essay: children, animals, trees, music, sunshine, rainbows, colors, dessert. She pinned the paper onto her bulletin board with a ladybug pin and stood back to look at it.

How stupid! she thought, disgusted with herself.

Ida was still hungry. She returned to the kitchen and sat down on the floor to investigate the lower cupboards on the right-hand side near the door. She hadn't looked in there in a long time and hoped there might be Wheat Thins or Cheez-Its. But no such luck. What she found instead was a large, clear plastic jar with a bright yellow top, crammed full of green olives.

Ida remembered these olives!

There had been a snowstorm when Dad had gotten a call from an old friend from his village who was in town and wanted to visit. When the man came to the door, Ida greeted him politely and escaped with her sisters to her parents' bedroom to watch TV. They found it boring to sit around while their parents talked about Palestine, especially when they talked in Arabic using adult words about adult ideas, which they barely understood.

She remembered seeing the jar with the olives on the table after the man left. Mom was crying, and Ida was scared that the man had hurt her. But Dad explained that Mom's older sister, Malayka—the one who had sent

Escape?

Ida the Arabic pendant—had cured the olives before she passed away a few months earlier in a car accident. Mom's brother, Jubran, had sent the jar of Malayka's olives with the visitor as a gift to Mom. And there they were—Aunt Malayka's green olives—still unopened in the cupboard. Simple, round, green olives.

Ida braced the plastic jar between her knees to twist off the top. She peeled away the clear cellophane underneath and found a layer of lemons and peppers and finally smallish, matte green olives. They were a bit slimy but she was too lazy to get up to rinse them off. She popped a few into her mouth. The flavor was pungent, distant, but somehow familiar. Famished, she chewed too fast, hit a hard olive pit, and heard a loud crack. She didn't break a tooth, but the sound made Ida wince and close her eyes. When she opened them, something felt different.

The click of a door lock made Ida jump as if she'd been caught doing something wrong. It was too early for the family to be home, but it sounded like a whole football team pushed its way into the apartment. Ida heard her mother call out, "We're home, my beauty!" Then Salwa bounded in and saw the olive jar. "I want some," she said with the whiny tone of someone who'd been left out when the candy was divided. *Is Salwa speaking Arabic?* Before Ida could comment, Salwa's little hand shot into the olive jar and pulled out a handful.

"Wash your hands first!" yelled Mom, exasperated.

43

"You've been on a filthy bus!"

Mom leaned over and kissed Ida on the forehead.

"How was school?"

Ida's mouth opened, but she couldn't answer. She stared at her mother and felt dizzy.

Mom's face was the same and her body was the same. But she was wearing tight, black polyester pants that flared at the bottom and a green print blouse with a black vest over it, although Ida clearly remembered that Mom had left that morning wearing her favorite jeans and white tailored blouse with her favorite black sweater. But most shocking was her head! She wore a black scarf tightly over her hair, with a green scarf matching her blouse more loosely covering her head and neck.

Before Ida had time to figure out what she was seeing, she noticed Salwa, who had now taken over the olive jar and was sitting next to Ida on the floor shoving them into her mouth. Everything about her was different! She wore a dark blue polyester school uniform instead of the Princess Jasmine sweatshirt she'd worn every day for more than a year now. The uniform was a sort of sleeveless apron over a light blue shirt and dark pants, and had a school patch on the left. Her hair was tied back severely instead of flowing in perfect, long ringlets that invariably caused at least two old ladies to stop her and say, "What I wouldn't pay for your curls!" every single time they went out in public.

Without thinking, Ida stood up and steadied herself on the kitchen table. *When did we put a table in the kitchen?* She noticed the kitchen was bigger, the walls white-washed and the floors made of cold tile. In a daze, Ida moved to the large window that overlooked the street hoping to see a familiar jam of cars rushing home from downtown to the western suburbs where houses were farther apart and kids played in their backyards instead of the street. But though she touched the window gently as she always did, that wasn't the scene that greeted her on the other side. This was definitely not Oldbridge, Massachusetts.

There were concrete buildings everywhere, mostly three and four stories tall, but some were taller. They weren't all facing the street or lined up next to one another like they were supposed to. Instead, they were squeezed in anywhere they fit, jostling for territory like hungry children in a school lunch line. Most of the buildings had balconies on which sheets and pants and socks hung brazenly from laundry lines. The only color, except the gray and brown of the concrete buildings and dirt roads, came from the pale green, yellow and blue plastic grocery bags that had been tucked into the nooks and crannies of chain link fences by the hot wind playing hide-and-seek with the trash in the street. This was not Oldbridge, but something about it was familiar...

Across the road was a huge soccer field, brown and rocky, with patches of green weeds. It seemed to belong to a school just above it on a hill. There were boys—it looked like thousands of them—streaming out of the school and hanging around in the field. Others talked and fooled around casually as they crossed the street, tying up traffic as far as she could see in both directions. And the people... *Who are those people?* Ida had no idea.

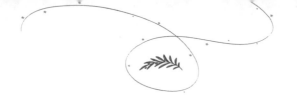

Wait! Ida had seen this scene in a picture!

Ida gasped as she remembered the black and white photo on the first page of mom's small album. Carolina had noticed the perspective—the photo was taken from an upstairs window looking down on a village. But this place didn't look like an old-fashioned farming village. It looked like a chaotic little city.

Could this be Busala, the place where my parents were born and lived until they moved to the States? She wondered.

The road just below the window was paved, but the edges were uneven and there were no sidewalks. It went up to the left to an intersection that had no stoplight. From there, cars went left, but Ida couldn't see from the window where that road led. The road to the right at that intersection seemed to wind its way up the hill to where the school stood. The street continued straight, too, to what looked like a commercial district with busses parked haphazardly, contributing to the traffic congestion. Down to the right, the road wasn't paved, but it was wide enough for two cars to pass. Rocks and piles of trash and occasional parked cars marked the edges. From the window, Ida couldn't see or guess what lay at the end of that road.

✦ ✦

Ida was vaguely aware that someone was moving from the refrigerator to the stove to the sink and back to the table. Then she felt tender hands on her shoulders, as her mother guided her away from the window and planted her in a seat at the kitchen table in front of a plate piled with chicken and vegetables. Her stomach rumbled so loudly, she ought to have woken from her strange dream, but nothing changed.

Sitting to her left, in her regular spot, Ida saw Danya. She had the same long face, wavy brown hair and mysterious eyes, but she didn't wear a permanent scowl as if she had gotten stuck in her family by losing a bet. She looked relaxed, pretty. Next to her, Salwa ripped a piece of pita bread and used it to pry chicken meat off the bones. Her skin, always tan, looked even darker than usual. Mom passed the rice to Dad who was sitting in his spot to Ida's right. Ida noticed he was wearing an embarrassingly bright green workout outfit with fake Nike logos on top and bottom (the logo said "Nikke!").

Her head hurt. Badly.

Mom sat down in the chair where she always sat and smiled at her family as if everything were normal. Dad raised a spoon and spoke in his familiar, loving voice, but in Arabic.

"So, girls, how was your day?"

He was looking straight at Ida.

5

"Fly Like a Bird!"

"Time to wake up, *habibti*, or you'll be late for school, my love!"

Ida groaned when Mama sang her awake as she always did. Ida was not a morning person.

She felt the brazen sun accost her through the window and knew something was very wrong. Her eyes shot open, and her body froze. Mama was still speaking Arabic. To her surprise, Ida could still understand it perfectly. She was still in Busala.

Ida sat up and reached instinctively for Mama, who sat down on the edge of the bed and wrapped herself around Ida to warm her up. Ida felt confused. Mama was the only one who could help her when she felt scared, but now Mama was part of what was scaring her. She smelled the same, like fresh sage, but other than that, the whole

49

world had turned upside down. Ida felt lonelier than she did in the summer between first and second grades when she went to summer camp thinking that Carolina would be there only to find that Carolina was in another group. *Carolina! Where is Carolina now?* Did she notice that Ida was missing?

Mama and Danya went to the kitchen to make breakfast (Danya was cooking?) and Salwa was brushing her teeth, so Ida was alone in the room they all shared. She dressed in the school uniform that she found waiting, ironed and folded, at the end of her bed. She sat down to think.

Am I dreaming? Am I being punked? Or could it be that my parents didn't move to the United States in the first place?

Ida and her family ate hard boiled eggs sprinkled with salt, and dipped fresh pita bread into honey from the neighbor's hives, and thick yogurt *labne* with olive oil. They drank sweet tea with fresh mint floating on the top. And although she ate a lot, the food didn't give her a tummy ache the way pancakes and cheese omelets sometimes did.

Ida left the house with her sisters. She seemed to know where she was going, but she stayed close to them just in case. They walked toward the girls' school at the far end of the village. There was another school, mixed boys and girls, but Baba said it was backward: "Too much religion and not enough thinking!" According to Baba, the principal of the girls' school was more open-minded. She cared about developing girls as people, not just memorizing facts. Baba was the sports teacher at the boys' school in Busala, just like he was the phys ed teacher in Oldbridge. But even though he was a teacher, he looked sad when he talked about the schools in Palestine. "You kids deserve better," he'd tell them.

The three sisters walked in the street because cars were parked along the side of the road where the sidewalk should have been and, occasionally, there was a huge green garbage dumpster that stuck far out into the street, creating an obstacle course.

"Why is there trash all over the ground around the dumpster when the dumpster isn't even full?" Ida said aloud, in Arabic, though asking herself.

Danya thrust her hands into the air imitating that ambiguous expression Dad used, which Ida interpreted as, "What's wrong with people?"

"Danya, look! People have hung bags of bread on the metal handles of the dumpster. Why would they do that?"

At the sound of Ida's voice, several cats jumped out of the dumpster and scattered.

"It's *haram*, forbidden, for Muslims to throw bread into the trash. Bread is life," Danya explained patiently.

"Isn't it also *haram* to hang bread on the trash dumpster?" Ida retorted, scrunching up her nose at the stink of rot.

Danya threw her hands into the air with the same expression of utter disbelief, making Ida laugh. Ida usually only smiled and almost never laughed. It felt great.

Cars spouting clouds of exhaust appeared to dodge one another effortlessly as they drove too fast to wherever they were going. The people walking, even very small children,

seemed to somehow evade the cars without speeding up or changing course. Ida watched with fascination as a car reversed out of an alleyway and all the way down to the next corner, indifferent to the school children who were forced out of the way. Danya didn't talk much, but Ida sensed talking wasn't necessary. Even though the setting seemed strange, Danya felt close, not remote and detached as she usually was. Meanwhile, Salwa shuffled through the loose dirt between her two older sisters.

Girls came out of their buildings or down the side streets carrying heavy backpacks. Ida and her sisters greeted some and ignored others, occasionally commenting on someone's new haircut or shoes. Danya and Ida took turns reaching out to grab Salwa when she skipped away into the street or bumped into a street vendor selling freshly baked, sesame-covered Jerusalem *ka'ak*. No amount of explaining seemed to convince Salwa to behave, but Ida noticed none of the other kids her age were behaving either.

A few blocks down, Danya took Ida's arm without a word, pulling her toward the still-closed shops to what could barely be called a sidewalk. At first, Ida thought Danya was trying to avoid a group of boys coming toward them, apparently on their way to the boys' school. But the group of boys also casually swerved to the side. And as the boys and girls stood in a loose circle, Ida noticed that Danya was blushing.

"Hi, Basel. Hi, Mohammed, Mohammed and Hamoudi," Danya ventured.

A giggle erupted from Ida, and Danya shot her a look.

How can Danya not think it's hysterical to run into two guys named Mohammed and one named Hamoudi, which is just a nickname for Mohammed? Ida thought.

"What do you have today?" Basel asked Danya.

"Just a science test. You?"

"Math and geography," Basel answered, keeping his eyes on Danya.

"You're taking him to school with you?"

Danya teased, motioning with her head at Faris, Basel's three-year-old brother, who was holding his hand.

Ida was grossed out. The boy's pants were too long, and they were frayed at the bottom. His nose needed to be wiped. It wasn't yet eight in the morning, and Faris was already eating a bag of cheese puffs, crumbs all over his face and jacket. It confirmed to Ida that little kids are disgusting no matter what country they're in.

"I'm taking him to kindergarten," Basel said, embarrassed, as Faris started to whine and pull away.

"Good luck," Danya answered coyly, turning back toward the street.

"You too," Basel called softly, his friends looking at him with envy.

Ida couldn't believe it. Danya liked a boy! His name was Basel—and he was cute! What's more, Ida was in on Danya's a secret.

Smiling to herself, Ida ran to catch up with Salwa who had reached the intersection near the school and looked like she was going to cross with all the other kids who also weren't paying any attention to the passing cars. Ida caught

herself thinking that people in the States were more careful than Palestinians, but, in the same moment, she realized that it might not be so simple. In Oldbridge, cars and pedestrians followed rules and paid attention to lights and signs. Here, cars dodged people and people dodged cars. They paid attention to each other. It was different, but was it really less safe?

The sisters entered the school on a wave of pushing girls that dispersed into the yard. Ida lost Danya and Salwa, but she didn't feel the least bit scared or lonely, or that sense of dread she carried around when she was at school in Oldbridge. There were kids everywhere, and even though they bumped and jostled, they somehow harmonized, and Ida felt, perhaps for the first time, that she actually fit in.

⋆ ⋆

The school building was relatively new but felt bare in comparison to Riverview in Oldbridge. The girls' school in Busala was all concrete and the sound of stomping and talking (and yelling by teachers at students telling them to stop stomping and talking) reverberated off the walls. The wide stairways were crowded with lines of students pushing up one side and down the other. Ida somehow knew where she was going. But along with the familiarity was an aching that felt like homesickness, which didn't make any sense since she was, apparently, home. As they walked, girls caught her eye and waved and smiled as if Ida was actually popular.

The classroom was big and rectangular and well lit by the sunlight streaming through the big windows that lined one entire wall. Twenty desks were set in rows, each desk big enough for two students sitting side by side. Along one wall were metal bookshelves with the girls' books piled according to subject. The back wall was decorated with students' drawings of the human body (except the private parts) with the organs labeled in English in big, clear print. The open windows let in the sounds of teaching and playing from the other classrooms that surrounded the yard, which mixed with the screechy sound of the metal desks and chairs on the marble floor as the girls got ready for class.

"Move over!" a girl said gruffly as she pushed Ida into a seat and then sat down next to her.

Tears sprung to Ida's eyes.

Another girl with thick, long braids had picked up the pile of Arabic handwriting books from the metal shelves and was handing them out. She got to Ida's desk and bent down to show off her beautiful gold hoop earrings. Ida was startled. She smiled, and the girl slipped a stick of gum into the pages of Ida's handwriting book. Ida glanced around and saw several other girls smiling at her and showing her their gum without letting the teacher see.

Ida was in on it! She started to unwrap the gum, but before she did, she ripped it and gave half to the girl sitting at the desk with her. The girl looked taken aback, but took the gum anyway and slipped it into her mouth.

Arabic class was bearable because of the secret messages exchanged among the girls. The messages weren't important—just notes about what the teacher was wearing (way too much eye makeup) or what happened on a TV

show the previous day (Jamal couldn't divorce his wife until he proved that her claim to be pregnant was a lie)—but it was fun trying to avoid the suspicious eyes of the teacher. Ida was called a goody-goody at home.

"Did I say you could pass notes?" boomed the teacher when she caught sight of a note making its way from the back of the room.

She was so loud that Ida's ears actually hurt. In Oldbridge, the teachers raised their voices sometimes. But screaming like that would have brought the principal running followed by complaints from parents, and maybe even a school community meeting.

This place is really strange, Ida thought.

The girl in the seat next to Ida stood up suddenly in a threatening posture.

"You didn't say we couldn't!"

"I'm saying it now," mocked the teacher, in an equally threatening stance. "And I'm telling *you* to go to the principal right now."

That's not fair! The note wasn't anywhere near her, thought Ida. But she was too chicken to defend her deskmate.

"You can't punish me for doing something that you never said I couldn't do," Ida's deskmate repeated.

She looked smug, pleased with herself for using such sound logic. Ida imagined how this girl, her expression and her attitude would get kids in Oldbridge calling *her* a terrorist—and they'd be so wrong! This girl was acting out, yes, but she was just a kid.

"Watch me," the teacher spat.

She pulled the girl past Ida, who cringed in sympathy, and out the door. All you could hear until the period ended was the scratching of pencils on the Arabic handwriting books. Ida couldn't tell if her classmates were even breathing.

Ida closed her book and marveled that her handwriting in Arabic wasn't half bad. She felt sure that Dad would be proud. "In our culture," he would say, "you have to pay attention to how things look to others. People will judge you based on appearance, not just substance."

Ida thought about her deskmate, who was certainly being punished, and wondered who she was trying to impress with her fearlessness, and why she practically volunteered to get in trouble, when the teacher had caught another girl with the note. Ida found out later that the girl who got caught with the note was her deskmate's twin sister, and it all made sense.

⋆⋆⋆

Another teacher came in to teach civics. She was very young, perhaps a recent graduate, and was all dressed up like she was going to a job interview. She wore a tailored jacket over pressed slacks that tucked into her shiny black leather boots, and an attractive two-tone headscarf. At first, she didn't seem too confident. She kept looking in the book, reading out the directions, and checking the book again to be sure she had read the directions correctly. Once the class got going, though, the teacher seemed to be having as much fun as the kids. They measured and traced various lengths and widths

on construction paper, cut and folded them, and taped them into three-dimensional shapes and laid them on a big piece of cardboard to make it look like a city.

Unlike the Arabic teacher, the civics teacher seemed happy to be teaching. She squealed when the girls cut and taped correctly, and she was patient when they were imprecise and the shape didn't fit together properly. It took a few minutes of thinking, but Ida finally remembered what they were doing in civics class in Oldbridge—recycling. They had been required to figure out two pages of questions about how many trees were needed to make a certain amount of paper, and how much paper was needed for various school activities, and how much paper could be recycled for how much money, which would save how many trees, and that would sink how much carbon from the atmosphere. In comparison, cutting and taping shapes seemed like baby work that Salwa could do, and who cared anyway?

Ida tried to reconcile all her conflicting feelings—she wanted to be invisible, and she wanted to be seen. She wanted schoolwork to matter and she didn't want it to be hard. She wanted to go home, but she wasn't sure where home was.

✦ ✧

After snack time, the English teacher came in. She wore a huge gold cross around her neck along with a bunch of other gold chains and bracelets that covered her entire lower arm making a clinking sound when she moved slowly and a clanging sound when she moved quickly. Ida panicked.

If the teacher realized how good her English was, she might be found out (found out for what, she wasn't sure). *I can't say a word!* Ida was thinking so hard that she worried the teacher might even hear her thoughts.

There was some confusion as the English books were distributed. Apparently, they weren't in the right order and every single girl wanted to grab at the pile to find hers. Ida tried to use the confusion to find some way out of the room, but she couldn't think fast enough. Anyway, where could she go?

Even before all the students had opened to page fifty-five, the teacher started to yell at a girl in the front to read aloud. Ida couldn't figure out why the teacher was yelling, but no one else seemed to consider it strange. Each girl read a sentence or two, but it was impossible to hear what they were saying because the teacher was yelling the sentence at the same time, as if they weren't doing what she had asked.

"Higher your voice!" the teacher shouted when she wanted a girl to speak more loudly, which made Ida giggle.

When it was her turn, the teacher yelled along and didn't hear a word Ida said anyway.

✢ ✢

Before they left to go down to the yard for exercise, the teacher reminded them to interview an elder about their memories of the village and come prepared to talk in class about what they learned.

Another presentation!

Ida looked frantically among her classmates for someone like Carolina who would understand the panic that was coursing through her body, but there was no one. Then her eyes found the window and her gaze settled on the brown hills beyond the village boundaries, hills that had survived so much more than stupid presentations, and Ida felt herself calming down.

⋆ ⋆

The girls stood in line in the yard until it was their turn to somersault on the mat and jump on one foot through four neon hula-hoops on the ground.

"Did you cut your hair?" one girl said to another, playing with the girl's ponytail.

"Yes, I'm going to a wedding on Friday," the girl answered with obvious excitement. "My father's cousin is marrying a girl from Jordan. I already got to see her and she looks like a princess even without the white veil." Then she added, "My auntie even got me a new dress for the wedding—at the mall!" before jumping onto the mat and somersaulting rather hard onto her back.

"Did you know that Layla is sick?" another girl said to Ida while they waited for their turn. "That's why she wasn't in school yesterday or today."

"Oh no. What does she have?"

Ida was past the age when children think it's fun to be sick so that they can miss school.

"Her cousin told me that it's called 'arthritis.' Something that hurts your knees and elbows. The doctor told Layla that she's going to have it all her life!"

Ida opened her mouth to say how terrible that was. But it was her turn, so she somersaulted on the mat and gracefully hopped through the hoops. On the other side, the girls were lining up against a concrete wall waiting for the teacher to tell them what to do next, and Ida joined them as if it were something she had done many times. The teacher, wearing a *jilbab*, one of those full-body coats that some Muslim women wear for modesty, looked comical as she did a few clumsy jumping jacks for the girls to follow. Then, she appeared to have run out of ideas and suddenly shouted, "Fly like a bird!"

The girls must have done this before because, without any prodding, one ran forward with her arms stretched out and the others followed, laughing and flapping. Ida took her place and ran, self-consciously at first. But then she seemed to forget where she was and who she was with. Her arms became feathers and her legs grew light. Lifted by the warm, dry currents, Ida felt herself rise above the yard, above the school, above her fears and questions. She flew left, at one with the flock, inhaled her history and blended into the cloudless blue sky. Below, her family's steadfast village seemed to call, "*Khaliki*. Stay forever." Ida swooped low over the almond and fig tress crammed into tiny plots between buildings. She greeted the pigeons that lived in the crevices of the high concrete roofs.

Ida fluttered and glided, feeling a profound sense of peace.

★ ☆

When Ida and her sisters got home from school that day, Mama was putting a huge platter of stuffed grape leaves on the table.

"My favorite!" Ida cried, feeling at home in every way.

Mama smiled knowingly.

"You're the greatest Mama ever," Ida said unthinkingly, as she had said a million times before.

"And you're the greatest Ida ever," Mama said, as she had said a million times before.

6
A Gift

Danya shook Ida out of a deep sleep.

"Get up, *ya kaslana!*"

She always called Ida lazy, even though Ida was sure that Danya was the lazy one.

"I'm starting in the kitchen. Don't make me do your share of cleaning or you'll pay," Danya said as she left the room, but without even a hint of her usual meanness.

Fridays were a special prayer day—no school!—but for women and girls in Busala, Fridays were reserved for cleaning house. *Would it really be so horrible to sleep in, even a little?* Ida groaned to herself. She stretched under the scratchy cover and pondered how her hard-to-pronounce-name and frizzy hair were all normal here, and she wondered for the gazillionth time what the heck was going on.

Why am I here?

For the first time, the question didn't frighten her. She just sat up and listened to the stillness in the village, and to the stillness inside her own head.

But then she remembered that she would be visiting her grandparents today, and it made her stomach feel funny. On the one hand, she was supposed to interview an elder about old times in Busala, and Ida hoped she might find someone to help her. On the other hand, so far, she hadn't been found out for being an outsider. But what if someone asked a question that she should be able to answer, and couldn't? What if she didn't know the proper way to act and everyone laughed? Or got angry?

Ida got dressed and wandered to the kitchen where her mother was frying Arabic cheese in a pool of olive oil for breakfast. Ida had always loved the crispy edges, but today she barely touched it.

✦ ✧

For the next three hours, Ida and Danya went from room to room wiping every single picture frame, perfume bottle, and knickknack. There was a thin coat of dust on everything. Even Salwa tried to help. She enjoyed spraying blue cleaner on the windows and swirling it around with newspaper until it made a big mess that one of the older girls had to go and wipe clear so that it shined.

"Come drink some juice!" Mama called from the kitchen.

Ida loved fresh orange juice, but no one ever had time to squeeze it in Oldbridge, even though they had an electric juicer and here they just used a plastic hand juicer. She swished the sweet and tart taste of Palestinian oranges around in her mouth and remembered her father telling her how Yaffa, a city on the Mediterranean coast, was famous for its oranges. Now she understood why.

"It's hot today," Danya complained, bringing Ida back from her faraway thoughts.

"Hot enough for ice cream?" Salwa asked with excitement.

"Okay," Mama caved immediately. "But eat it on the stairs outside so you don't drip in here while we're cleaning."

She put some coins in Salwa's hand and pushed her out of the kitchen.

It all seemed so strange! Mama sending Salwa to the store? By herself? And to buy ice cream—before lunch? These were the same people, but different. And Ida herself felt the same, but also different.

At home in Oldbridge, Ida would do anything to get out of cleaning. There was even a family joke that whenever Mom asked for help, Ida would suddenly feel sick, or remember some important homework assignment she'd forgotten to do, or need to go to the bathroom for a really long time. Surprisingly, Ida was realizing that cleaning could be fun when the whole family did it together.

They rolled up all the carpets and draped them over the wall of the balcony. Ida could see maroon and blue fake Turkish carpets hanging from balcony after balcony across the village, like pine nuts and almonds garnishing jasmine rice.

They rolled up the hems of their pants legs and put on plastic house shoes so they wouldn't slip. Mama filled a bucket with warm water and suds, and poured it out on the floor. With a squeegee on the end of a broomstick, each girl swept the water around the floor, into the corners, and then into a big drain in the far corner of the room. They scrubbed from room to room, until the house was sparkling and smelled of bleach. With bright sun and a steady breeze caressing the clean house, it felt like a fresh start, a new beginning.

⁺✦ ☆⁺

Ida bathed Salwa, and then herself in the trickle of water that came from the bathtub tap and dressed them both in shiny clothes that people in Busala considered fancy, but that many of her classmates at Riverview would have found ugly. By noon, they were all ready to leave for their grandmother and grandfather's place, reigniting Ida's nerves.

What do I know about my Sitti and Siddo? Ida racked her brain.

Ida knew that her dad loved his mother, but he never really talked about her very much.

Guilt overtook Ida as she realized that she never asked any questions about *Sitti*. What was she like?

Ida did have an impression of her grandfather. She sensed from her Dad that *Siddo* was traditional and closed-minded and harsh, although her father would not have used those words. Her mother always said that *Siddo* was very loving "in his own way." It was funny, but Mom had always seemed closer to Dad's family than Dad was himself, maybe because she had lost her own father to diabetes when she was not yet ten, and her mother died soon after, apparently from a broken heart.

⋆⁺ ⋆⁺

Ida let the others leave the house ahead of her, unsure where she was going and unsure whether she really wanted to get there. She was surprised when instead of going down the stairs to the street to where the car was parked, they marched in a big procession *up* the stairs to the second floor of the two-story building.

Bursting in without even knocking, Danya and Salwa ran first to the kitchen, where they found *Sitti* hovering over a pot of chicken soup, the smell of carrots and potatoes steaming up the windows. She was Ida's height, maybe even a little shorter, and the flowing tent-dress covered with triangles didn't help to hide her extra width. Despite the heat in the kitchen, she wore a tight-fitting, black hijab covering her head and neck.

Sitti wiped beads of sweat from her forehead and reached out, still holding the big stirring spoon.

"Peace be upon you, *Sitti*," her grandmother said to Danya in that funny way that the grown-ups called children by the name that the children called them. She kissed Danya on both cheeks and moved on to Salwa.

"Peace be upon you, *Sitti*," her grandmother said to Salwa.

Sitti greeted Ida the same way and returned to the stove without waiting for an answer.

"*Alaykum a-Salam*," Ida called after her, returning the blessing.

The girls turned and walked respectfully to the main room, left their shoes in the huge pile near the door, and went to greet their grandfather.

"*Marhaba Siddo*," Danya said, wishing him good morning as she shook his hand, moving on without a pause. On the corner sofa, six of her girl cousins sat cramped together in their Friday clothes, pushing one another, giggling, and sharing small toys stashed in their pockets. The boys were outside chasing each other through the alleys between the buildings, scuffing their shiny black Friday shoes.

Salwa went straight to the cousins' couch without even greeting her *Siddo*. Ida panicked that he would think that Salwa was acting disrespectfully. But her grandfather didn't seem to care at all, and instead of getting mad, *Siddo* chuckled and shouted, "Hello to you, too!" in Salwa's direction.

When it was Ida's turn, *Siddo* pulled her close, with a strong hand on the back of her head, kissed her on the right cheek and then the left, and gave her a warm hug. *Siddo* smelled of the same woody aftershave that her dad used.

Although she'd had the impression from Dad that *Siddo* wasn't nice, Ida was sure now that there was nothing scary in this house. *Siddo* would be the perfect person to help her with her school assignment.

"Is that a new blouse?" Jana, one of the younger cousins, asked Ida when she reached the growing gaggle of girls.

She fingered Ida's shiny buttons.

"I guess so."

"How much was it?" Mira, another cousin, chimed in.

"Um, I don't know."

"My mom got *me* three new blouses on sale for one hundred shekels," Jana bragged, not only to Ida but to the whole gang of cousins.

"My Mama got me *four* new blouses for one hundred shekels," Mira responded.

Mira was tiny. *Sitti* said it was because she had been kissed too many times on the soles of her feet when she was a baby.

"Well, *my* Mama got *me* five new blouses and a belt for one hundred shekels!" another cousin jumped in.

She couldn't have been more than four years old.

"I don't believe you! I'm gonna ask your Mama," Jana shouted, running toward the kitchen where all the aunties had gathered to help prepare the meal.

The whole crowd of girls ran to the kitchen, each trying to reach her mother first. But before they got to the kitchen, there was a roar of bangs and claps, which diverted the other girls to the balcony to see what was going on while Ida ran for cover behind a door.

"What was that?" she asked, afraid she might faint.

"Fireworks, silly," a cousin explained. "There must be a wedding today."

Ida was relieved. But for a few moments, the magic of being together with so much family was broken.

I want to go home, she thought to herself.

✦ ✧

Sitting on a tablecloth spread on the kitchen floor, the kids ate a huge meal prepared by *Sitti* and the aunties, while Danya, as the oldest cousin, presided over them, scolding them when they fought and refilling the plates of tahini-covered lamb *kuftah* meat fingers, fried eggplant sloshed in tomato sauce, and red cabbage salad, as if she were one of the mothers.

"These are the best pickles I've ever tasted!" Ida exclaimed at the sour burst of flavor.

Ida remembered how her dad used to say that Palestinian pickles fermented with garlic were so much tastier than the vinegar-soaked dill pickles from the grocery store in Oldbridge. Fortunately, there was too much chewing and clanging and joking for anyone to pay any attention to Ida's silly remark.

In the other room, *Siddo* sat at the head of a long plastic table.

"Bring more pickles for the far end of the table," he told *Sitti*, and she got up at once to get more.

"We're fine, *haj.*"

Baba spoke to his father using the respectful term for a man who had completed the Muslim pilgrimage to Mecca, even though *Siddo* hadn't.

"There are plenty of pickles—look!" an uncle motioned to the small plates, nearly full, sitting in front of each person.

"Pickles are healthy!" *Siddo* insisted." They're packed with vitamins A, C, K and *gimmel, yod, dalet*," he joked, throwing random Hebrew letters in with the English ones.

A Gift

Sitti quietly rolled her eyes as she topped off the pickle plates. Ida remembered that expression! It was the same amused, forgiving and almost maternal look that Mom wore when Dad complained that she had interrupted his precious soccer game. Ida imagined this was a face that women in Busala kept in their pocket to pull out when their men acted silly.

As the meal went on, *Siddo*'s four sons and their wives all treated him with extra respect. Before he could ask, they handed him the dishes, even when they were already within his reach. They nodded and agreed with whatever he said. When he was completely wrong, it was Ida's father who would fill in the silence in a gentle way, saying, "Well, *haj*, these days, some people who know a lot have different ideas about that."

Ida noticed that *Siddo* always seemed to listen carefully to her father and take to heart what he said.

After lunch, *Siddo* headed for the couch where he rested after meals, but Ida approached him awkwardly.

"*Siddo*? Would you help me with my schoolwork and tell me what you remember about Busala in the old days?"

"I'll help, if I can," he assured her.

Siddo had only gone to school through the fourth grade. Everything he knew, he'd learned from reading the Muslim holy book, the *Quran*, by listening to his elders, and through his own hard life.

"We'll go outside," he said.

⋆⋆ ⋆

Ida walked downstairs with *Siddo* and behind the building, where there was a small bit of land that he tended along a wall that marked the border with the neighbor's property. *Siddo* walked up to one of the fruit trees and picked two ripe loquats, *askadinya*. He put one small orange fruit into his mouth and handed the other one to Ida . It was sweet but slightly sour, with the texture of a plum. *Siddo* threw the pit under a tree, so Ida did the same.

He walked over to a plot of seedlings and Ida followed.

"My cucumbers," *Siddo* said. He bent down on one knee to check the tender sprouts just starting to break through the cracked ground.

"In a couple of months, God willing, these will be vines, heavy with cucumbers that your *Sitti* will turn into pickles," he said.

Ida stepped back and gazed at the little plot. The neat, small squares, each one dedicated to a different vegetable, and the fruit trees all in a graceful line, made her feel calm. And there was the upholstered armchair, under the lemon tree, where *Siddo* took his afternoon naps when it was warm enough.

"It's a beautiful garden, *Siddo*," Ida said.

"But not like the farm I remember from when I was a child." he replied. There was hurt in his voice.

Siddo still considered himself a farmer, even though he hadn't farmed since the villagers' fields had been taken away from them.

As they stood in the cool shade of the trees, Ida's grandfather told her how their village's land had sprawled across three hilltops, and the valleys in-between. But now Israeli settlers and soldiers were everywhere, and it wasn't safe to go far from where people lived, especially not alone.

Siddo told her how, despite the threats and dangers, Busala families had always been able to live off the land. In the old days, he explained, each of the eight original families lived in their own big room built of straw, clay and stone clustered around the village well. Around the rooms, each family's farm was marked off by boulders as old as the land itself, and the plots spread across the valley like big prayer rugs. The olive groves reached up the mountainside and like the *mukhaddir*, who guarded the fields, they made everyone feel safe.

The most respected farmers were those whose rows of seeds were neat, each one tucked gently under a small mound of rich, fertile earth. They raised their olive trees with the care that mothers show to their babies. Even in the spring when there was no harvest, a good farmer kept the branches pruned, and they cleaned up the twigs at the base of the trunks as a mother picks up the scattered toys of a small child at the end of a day. *Siddo* said if he fulfilled his responsibility toward the trees, the trees would give back branches weighed down with olives when the time came.

In fact, when *Siddo* was young, and when his father was young, and when *his* father was young, men, women and children worked together to produce not only olives, but wheat, figs, cactus, grapes, tomatoes, cucumbers, watermelon and other fruits and vegetables. Families often produced more than they needed and were able to trade

or sell the surplus. The abundance of fresh, nutritious food was seen as a blessing from *Allah* and fair compensation for hard work.

As *Siddo* spoke, Ida could see herself encircled by the swishing skirts of women as they reached into trees to claim the small fruit. She could hear the rain-like pit-pat of olives hitting the tarps laid out under the trees. Through *Siddo's* steady voice, Ida could feel the dry, scratchy olive twigs under her feet and a dull ache in the small of her back from picking day after day in the harvest season with her cousins.

In the picture that *Siddo* painted of the old days, there were no borders and no military checkpoints dividing up the land. Shepherds wandered the Jerusalem hills with their flocks, grazing village common land, as generations of shepherds had done before. The women made creamy milk and cheese from the sheep and goats, and on special occasions, they sold meat to their neighbors, usually joining in the celebration of an Eid or wedding or birth.

Ida hung on every word knowing that what *Siddo* said was true because he remembered it in his bones.

Over the generations, a man's land was divided among his wife and children according to the rules spelled out in the *Quran* and some people sold to other families or outsiders who had moved in, until the families lived all mixed up and they farmed side-by-side. And then the British came, and more Jewish immigrants, until the establishment of the State of Israel on what used to be Palestine.

Palestinians called it the *Nakba*, "the catastrophe."

Ida knew that Palestinians had lost their homeland in 1948, because there was a big *Nakba* commemoration at the Palestinian community center near Oldbridge every year. She had found it boring listening to all the speeches. But hearing *Siddo* tell her about it made it interesting—and real.

"Slowly, more and more of Busala's land was taken over and made off-limits to us," *Siddo* said. "Then the Israelis took the land with the excuse that it wasn't being used. The village's boundaries shrank, but our families grew, and the closest fields had to be used for buildings to live in."

Ida thought about how today nearly every piece of Busala's land was crammed with buildings, and the surrounding fields were unplanted, unused, and unus-able, patrolled by soldiers who protected the new Jewish neighborhoods—settlements—that had sprung up on the hilltops that belonged to the village.

"Farmers are the ones that take care of the land of Palestine. The ones that care for the trees that our grand-fathers planted and their grandfathers before them," *Siddo* said.

"Be proud," he said, tapping Ida on the shoulder. "Be proud to belong to a family of *fellaheen*, farmers. So many of our people were driven away in 1948, when Israel was established and again during the war in 1967. But we stayed and will always stay on our land here in Palestine."

Siddo sighed deeply and seemed to fade into his mem-ories. There was a long, quiet pause.

"Are you okay, *Siddo*?" Ida asked.

He smiled weakly at her.

"Most of my grandchildren don't want to know about farming or food or taking care of the land. And my children don't want to hear about it anymore either."

"Why not?" Ida asked.

"Maybe they are embarrassed or think farmers are old-fashioned." *Siddo's* voice trailed away. "Now the young people go to school and study for professions. Look at your father—a teacher! Two of your uncles are nurses, and one runs a business. Even your Uncle Ahmed who lives in Jordan has a good job with the United Nations, in charge of security. Your aunties who moved away with their husbands to Sweden and Saudi Arabia also went to school. We made many sacrifices, and we didn't have the choices that were our right. But Palestinians have made a big mark on the world anyway. Why would anyone choose to farm, especially when farmers are constantly being attacked?"

Ida guided her grandfather, who suddenly looked exhausted, to his chair under the tree.

"We *are* proud of who we are, *Siddo*, and we're proud of you," said Ida. "It's just that it's sometimes hard to imagine how all those things that happened so long ago still matter today."

"It matters because there used to be peace here and there can be again. Do you think our lives were always like this?" he asked, gesturing with his arms as if circling the whole village. "I need you to remember our homeland, and keep on remembering after I'm gone."

For the next few minutes, *Siddo* told Ida funny stories about being young, like her. He told her how he fought with his brothers over who would stay to work in the fields under the hot sun and who would get to take the produce to the bustling market just outside Damascus Gate in the Old City of Jerusalem where they would see interesting people from faraway places, like Jericho, Amman, or even farther, many of them dressed in costumes with many layers and colors like proud roosters.

He told her about when, as a teenager, he first noticed his future bride, her *Sitti*, standing in line at the olive press in the village as she waited for her turn to fill jugs with the season's new, pure olive oil. Her eyes were dark green, like *molokhiyya*, the bitter leaf boiled into a gooey soup that children loved.

Their conversation was interrupted when Ida's smaller boy cousins started kicking a soccer ball in the small yard, and the pair headed inside to eat watermelon.

Ida wanted to thank *Siddo*, but all she could do was hold onto him extra tight. She kept thinking about *Siddo* for the rest of the afternoon. There was a lot to remember. He had given Ida a gift. And she would have to find a way to live up to it somehow.

7

Arabs Got Talent

The first spate of gunshots was far away. It was the middle of the night when Salwa, still asleep, climbed into bed with Ida, as if she was on autopilot. She wrapped herself around Ida, who was more than glad to have the company.

Of course, Ida knew that Palestine was under military occupation, but she hadn't grasped that real military troops with real guns actually came to the village, even forcing their way into regular people's houses, and without warning. Ida lay wide awake, heart pounding, haunted by images of broken glass raining down on her and her sisters.

Soon, Ida heard yelling. It wasn't Arabic or English, but she could understand some of the words. *Is that Hebrew?* she wondered.

Ida slipped out of bed quickly, without disturbing Salwa, and went to look for her parents. She found them

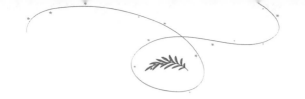

and Danya in the kitchen, sitting in the dark.

"Don't turn on the light!" Baba said harshly, as Ida moved toward the switch.

"We don't want to attract any attention," he said more softly, motioning for Ida to sit next to him.

Ida wasn't sure how long they had been talking in the dark.

"I don't understand, Baba," Danya was saying, obviously in the middle of a conversation.

Her voice was shaky.

"If they aren't going to demolish any houses tonight, why are they here?"

Mama poured Danya another cup of tea with extra sugar, and poured one for Ida, too.

Baba explained that many houses in the village were under demolition order. The Israelis would be knocking the houses down with bulldozers, along with whatever was in them, to make way for a parking lot. About twenty houses were slated for demolition, though it would likely end up being many more. The Israelis wouldn't want to park their cars in a lot surrounded by Palestinians. Since nearly all the buildings in their village had been constructed without building permits from the Israeli authorities, they were all vulnerable to demolition.

"They must have heard that youth in the village are preparing to fight them when they come. They came tonight to arrest a few boys and scare the rest of them into giving up their plans to resist," Baba explained.

Danya started to cry, and Ida froze, but Baba kept

talking like he didn't notice.

"You girls need to be very careful who you talk to. There are people in the village who are helping the Israelis. You can't always know who those people are. So don't trust anyone without being sure."

"Ayman, you're scaring them," Mama scolded, just before a woman's scream rang out across the field in front of the house.

"Let my son go—he didn't do anything!" the woman was shrieking. It sounded like Ida's aunt.

Baba moved quietly to the window. They heard glass breaking, water splashing and a woman cursing.

"The soldiers are taking one of Jubran's sons, maybe two of them."

He turned and looked at Mama.

"Soldiers?" Ida gasped.

"Well, they call themselves 'police' but that's a joke. They have military training, military weapons, and they're enforcing a military occupation. They're soldiers as far as we're concerned." Baba explained.

Ida felt every muscle in her body tense.

"Our house isn't going to be demolished, is it, Baba? This is our house. They can't come in here, right?"

Ida could barely get out a whisper.

He paused as if to start the story again from the beginning.

"Well, the land belongs to your grandfather, and I have the papers showing it was owned by *his* father and by *his* father before him."

"So, we're safe, right?"

"We should be. But you need a building permit from Israeli authorities. Everybody needs a permit to build, but they only give permits to Jewish Israelis. Many families in our village wasted years and spent all their money on lawyers and fees trying to get a building permit. They finally just built without a permit. So did we."

Mama rested her head on her hands, her teeth clenched in a way that Ida had never seen before.

"What's going to happen?" Danya finally worked up the courage to ask.

"I don't know, *habibti*," Baba sighed deeply. "But for now I want you two to promise not to let Salwa out of your sight. And keep these cell phones with you in case we need to reach you."

Baba took out two flip phones from his pocket and gave one to Ida and one to Danya.

Her first very own cell phone—Ida couldn't help but smile when she touched it!

"These aren't for talking to your friends," Mama smiled, when she saw the excitement flash across the girls' faces. "We want to be able to reach you if we need to. If you need to reach us, send a text message. It costs less than phoning."

✦ ✦
✦

The next morning, Baba was in the living room smoking, which he never did, and talking loudly on two cell phones at the same time. Mama didn't shush him to keep his voice down as she usually did. He scribbled notes in the margins of the newspaper spread out on the coffee table in front of him. He looked up when Ida and Danya appeared at the doorway in their pajamas. He had deep circles under his eyes, but he exuded a sense of strength, purpose.

"The police are gone. They got about fifteen boys, including your cousins Taher and Wassim. You girls go to school, and we'll know more when you get home."

Baba turned back to his phones. The girls, dazed, wandered to the kitchen for breakfast.

✦ ✦

It was a hard day at school. Ida was very sleepy. All the girls in her class were anxious. It was difficult to concentrate on anything, knowing that police and border guards and soldiers had been in the village and could show up again at any time. Even the adults were distracted, answering their phones during class time, going into the hallway to talk, leaving the girls sitting at their desks with their imaginations.

Ida wanted to understand more about what was going on. She tried to ask her teachers questions, but they, and her classmates, seemed to talk in slogans: "The Israelis aren't going to get our houses." Or "Those Americans should learn that we Palestinians are never going to give up our land."

Ida wished she had listened all those times her father had sat her and her sisters down to explain to them what the Palestinian cause was all about. It didn't seem real then. Now she was in the midst of it, still not understanding.

✦ ✦

83

"Danya?"

On the walk home from school, Ida tried to straighten out her thoughts.

Danya grunted, the same way Baba did when he wanted to show that he was listening but didn't feel like talking.

"I'm thinking about the people in other places, other countries," Ida continued.

"Okay."

"They probably don't know what is going on here... I mean, what's *really* going on."

"I guess."

"Maybe big, important people do. But not regular people, who just go to work or school every day and are busy with their own lives."

Ida was thinking about Fernando and Alberto, the guards in her building in Oldbridge, and the computer programmers who ate in Carolina's family's restaurant, and the ladies in Mom's zumba class at the YMCA, and that kid in her class named Daryl. Even her teachers who talked about peace and justice all the time probably didn't really know what it was like to live under a military occupation.

"A few might understand, but most all of them probably believe what they see only on TV."

Danya stopped walking so abruptly that Salwa, who was holding her hand, nearly lost her balance, and for a second Ida worried that she'd made her sister mad.

Danya looked straight at Ida.

"I bet you're right. Why don't you help tell them?" Danya said.

Does Danya actually believe in me? Ida wondered. *Could I tell people the truth? And if I did, would they even listen?*

The girls walked the rest of the way home without a word.

✦ ✧

Sitting at the kitchen table while Mama got ready to make dinner, Ida forced herself to finish her homework. It was useless busy work, not even worth the effort of color coding or checking it off her list. Salwa wasn't able to do her homework without help, so Ida sat next to her as she memorized a short *sura* from the *Quran*. Just as they finished, the doorbell rang, and Danya opened it.

"Auntie!" she said with unusual excitement.

"Angel!" answered a slightly husky voice, which was immediately muffled in a hug.

In a big whoosh, a large woman who smelled wonderfully of citrus dropped a ton of bags of food on the kitchen table and kissed Mama on the right cheek, then the left, then the right again. She kissed Ida on the nose and picked Salwa up and twirled her around on her shoulders. Mama laughed.

"Enough, Malayka!"

Ida choked.

It was her Aunt Malayka—Mama's older sister—who had died about six months ago! The one Mama loved more than the world itself! The one who gave Ida the pendant! The one who cured the olives!

Without resting for a second, Malayka went to the counter limping slightly. She took the lettuce, cucumbers, and tomatoes from Mama and started chopping. She popped a slice of cucumber into Salwa's mouth and stuck one into her own. She and Mama talked nonstop while the girls listened.

"So, what exciting places have you been to in the last couple of days?" Mama looked at her sister enviously.

"I went to Ayn Qinya to see those families."

Entire Bedouin families were being pushed out by settlers.

"It's a beautiful time of year to hike through the *wadi*, when water trickles through the riverbed beneath those rolling hills covered with wildflowers. I was wishing the whole time that you were with me, Somaya."

"Yes, well...."

"And remember the little girl with the green eyes? Majd? She asked about you."

"You know I'm not able to run around trying to save Palestine like you, Malayka."

The sharp click-click sound of the knife on the cutting board punctuated her words.

"And besides, it's getting more and more dangerous to get in and out of Busala. Didn't you see the armed guards on your way into the village?"

"Sure, I saw them. There's a permanent checkpoint at the entrance now. They're checking identity cards and searching cars."

Malayka seemed to remember that she was angry.

"Can you believe that I had to use my press pass to get in here? They wanted to keep me out of my own village!"

Malayka had an apartment in the city, and Busala had been closed to everyone whose identity card didn't list an address in the village.

"I only got in because I lied and said I was writing a story for *Haaretz*!"

"I'm surprised they didn't keep you out *because* you're writing a story," Mama countered.

"They don't want our stories in the media, but they also don't want the world to say they don't have a free press. Actually, I think it's just a matter of chance. One time you get an officer at the checkpoint who wants to show you he's the boss, so he doesn't let you in. The next time you get one that wants to show you how reasonable and fair he is, and he does let you in."

"Why did you risk it today?" Mama asked. "It's too hot here. The youth are preparing for a confrontation, and the armed forces came and arrested twenty *shebab* yesterday. They took Wisam and Taher!"

Mama, who back home always seemed so strong, held in her tears.

"I know, Somaya, Jubran called me. They'll be home this afternoon."

Malayka put her arms around Mama's shoulders, and Mama leaned on her.

"But in the midst of hardship, there is always joy!" Malayka said, brightening everyone's mood. "Isn't today someone's birthday?"

"You remembered, Auntie!"

Salwa jumped into Malayka's arms, wrapping her legs around Malayka's waist and giggling into her neck.

Salwa had been listening to the talk about soldiers and checkpoints and the demolition of Palestinian homes, and she seemed to understand it, at least as much as any just-turned eight-year-old could. Yet Salwa didn't look as scared as Ida felt. *Salwa is used to war*, Ida thought. *Salwa is used to it. But I'm not.*

"Do I have to be a clown *again* and put spaghetti in my hair?" Malayka asked, faking a look of horror.

"No, Auntie," Salwa laughed, already sounding more grown up. "I just want to eat pizza while we watch *Arabs Got Talent*. Tonight is the finals!"

"Whatever you want, *habibti*," Malayka promised her, reaching for the flour and bowls.

"You finish the salad, Danya. I'll do the pizza. Ida can set the table."

Malayka was taking charge, as usual.

"Oh! And guess what? I brought a chocolate butter-cream cake with chocolate chips from the Jewish bakery!"

A chorus of "oohs" and "aahs" rose up. Everyone loved chocolate cake from the Jewish bakery. They couldn't wait to finish dinner so they could have dessert.

✦ ✧

In front of the television, the family sunk into the old, stretched leather couch they had salvaged from the side-walk in French Hill, where Israelis often threw out perfectly good stuff. The windows were open, and they could hear *Arabs Got Talent* playing from the neighbors' houses, too.

A way-too-skinny Bahraini woman was reciting poetry. It was pretty, but they all agreed it was not enough to pass her to the next level of the competition. Then came a little Yemeni boy who walked right to center stage in front of all those people, on international TV, and started to do an amazing break dance. He twirled on his head and did handstands in odd positions as the studio audience went wild. Ida could not believe that anyone could be so brave.

If I had to get in front of a bunch of people and show them something about myself, they'd probably laugh at me, and I would die! Ida thought.

Then she remembered the passion project, and she felt a flood of relief that she wasn't in Oldbridge.

Mama set a hot homemade pizza on the coffee table in front of them, and Ida's stomach growled a loud thanks— *shukran!* Without taking her eyes off the Egyptian fire-eater who just got buzzed by the judges, Ida reached for a slice and took a bite. There was a loud crack, and she realized too late.

It was topped with Aunt Malayka's home-cured green olives—the magic ones.

II

8
"Mamma Mia"

Ida found herself once again in her small Oldbridge apartment. The slice of Dominoes' olive-topped pizza in her hand came into focus, along with the girls' favorite chocolate-cake-from-a-box sitting on the table. ABBA played aloud from the iPod in the living room: *"Mamma mia. Here I go again. My, my. I should not have let you go."*

Mom came out of the kitchen balancing several glasses of milk on her favorite glass tray decorated with multicolored Palestinian embroidery that Ida now recognized as her grandmother's handiwork. Mom was thinner and fit. Her arm muscles even popped out a little from doing so much zumba. Danya sat at the end of the table looking far away. But for once, Ida didn't feel angry at her, or even indifferent. She felt concerned. Danya looked like she needed the kind of best friend that only a sister could be, and Ida felt guilty that she'd never realized that before.

Salwa was barely recognizable as she played quietly in the living room with four of her school friends and one from the building. The games and singing from the birthday party were over, and the girls were sitting in a circle on the rug looking over the gifts that Salwa had gotten—some books, a kit for making candles, a photo album, tickets to the science museum (from Mom and Dad), and a Dora the Explorer science set with test tubes and food coloring to mix colors. Ida grinned as she imagined a time (soon) when Salwa would also be a friend, sharing secrets and dreams with her two older sisters, who would protect her and give her advice.

Part of Ida wanted to shout, "I'm home!" But was she? Would anyone even believe what she'd been through?

"Um, Mom?"

Ida's voice felt strange in English.

"What's wrong, angel? Are you sick?"

"Not sick, but I'm not hungry. Can I go take a shower?"

Both Danya and Salwa looked up suddenly, eyes wide in disbelief.

"You're always hungry!" Salwa blurted.

"And you *want* to take a shower? You *never* want to shower," said Danya, being hurtful on purpose.

Caught off guard, Ida answered in the same tone.

"Well, I do now!"

She quickly left the table and went straight to the bathroom. Ida ran the water in the shower to hide the sound of her sobbing. But then she felt guilty about wasting water, so she got in. Her tears mixed with the water from the shower, and she imagined herself dissolving down the drain, never to be seen again.

Ida's senses slowly brought her back to where she was—at home in Oldbridge. Now the water was hot, and the water pressure was strong, not like in Palestine where water was diverted to Jewish settlements. The towel was fluffy and soft, and the soap smelled like vanilla, not like the soap in Palestine, which had an overpowering smell of fake roses. She hadn't noticed those things before. She got out and dried, trying to avoid her reflection in the mirror.

If she saw herself, who would she see?

Ida went into her bedroom and closed the door. Lightheaded, she considered that she might have jet lag, but that seemed unlikely. She threw on a t-shirt and shorts, and lay her wet head down on the pillow, and sleep overcame her all at once.

In a dream, Ida saw herself walking on Salah-a-din Street, the main shopping area outside the Old City of Jerusalem, when she noticed a girl about Salwa's age, dressed in filthy, torn clothes, sitting against a store with her hand outstretched. Ida stopped abruptly and stared. *How could anyone leave a child alone to beg on a city street?* she asked herself.

Suddenly, in her dream, Aunt Malayka was standing next to her. She took Ida by the shoulders and looked at her. She seemed so real.

"Ida, listen to me."

"That poor girl. She's alone. We have to help her," Ida protested, pulling away.

"Yes, it's sad, but look across the street, Ida. See that old lady who's begging? You see she's sitting directly across from the girl?"

"I see her."

"That's her grandmother, Ida. They're begging together. For their family."

Ida exhaled.

"I'm glad she's not here alone. But she shouldn't be here at all. She's just a kid. She should be playing."

"You have a big heart, Ida," Aunt Malayka said. "Just like your mother."

In the dream, Ida walked toward the little girl and Malayka didn't follow.

"Hi. I'm Ida," she said.

The girl looked up and tried to catch her grandmother's eye for direction about what to do.

Ida sat down near her on the sidewalk, making sure not to block her view of her grandmother.

"*Shu ismik?*" she asked the girl's name as if it were just an ordinary conversation.

The girl didn't know how to respond, so she just sat there quietly, looking into her lap. She seemed anxious that Ida was distracting her customers.

"How long do you have to stay out here?" Ida asked. "It's starting to get cold, don't you think?"

"I'm okay. My *Sitti* got me some hot tea."

The girl moved the scarf covering her lap to reveal a

steaming cup of tea.

"Oh."

Ida felt a bit stupid.

"Do you need anything else? I mean, it doesn't look like too much fun sitting out here for hours."

The girl looked slightly offended and held out her hand. Ida stood up and moved sideways so that the girl's grandmother could see her fish out a ten-shekel coin from her pocket and give it to the girl.

"Bye," Ida said, realizing that she hadn't helped at all, feeling she couldn't ever matter in Palestine, where so much was wrong.

The girl just looked down at her lap and didn't answer. She was waiting for no one to be looking so she could sip her hot tea.

9

Ida in Wonderland

"Ida, *habibti*?" Mom tapped gently on the door. "Carolina is on the phone."

Ida startled awake, her heart pounding.

"Should I tell her you'll call her back?" Mom asked.

"No!" Ida spurted out, surprising herself. "I'll pick it up in here."

"Hey," Ida said, still disoriented.

"Hey. Whatcha doing?"

"I think I fell asleep," Ida confessed. "Today feels like the longest day of my life."

"Lazy," Carolina snorted.

"That's what Danya called me when..."

Ida wished she could tell Carolina about when Danya had called her *kaslana* in Palestine, and how she said it with love not irritation. She ached to tell Carolina how it felt to toss the *askadinya* pit under her grandfather's tree, knowing that new fruit might grow from it. And she desperately wanted to imitate Aunt Malayka's husky voice so that Carolina would understand how powerful she was, and how wise. But for some reason, Ida felt these things were too fragile to share, that if she told anyone, they might disappear in a puff of smoke.

"So, guess what?" Carolina let a bit of excitement slip into her voice. "My mom said we can go to an early movie if we're both ready for school. I'm done with my homework. Are you?"

Ida reached into the backpack that lay open on the floor next to her bed. She pulled out the notebook where she listed each assignment, with the due date next to it. Every single one had a blue check mark, except the one that said "Passion Project," which wasn't due for another week.

"I guess I'm done," Ida said, pushing the assignment out of her mind, or at least trying to.

"Let me ask my mom."

How did Carolina know that she needed someone to help keep her grounded in reality? Ida wondered.

"Tell her that my brother is coming along to look out for us. Then she won't have any excuse for saying no," Carolina suggested.

Ida and Carolina both knew what it was like to have immigrant parents who were worried their kids would be swallowed up and ruined by "evil American culture" which put too much value on looks and money and not enough on family.

A minute later, Ida told Carolina she'd be waiting downstairs in an hour. Ida had barely hung up the phone when Mom came in and closed the door behind her.

Mom sat down on the bed gently.

"Can I comb the knots out of your hair?"

Ida didn't have any knots in her hair, but her mom sensed that something was wrong.

Ida could only nod. She was trying not to cry again.

Mom picked up a small plastic bottle of olive oil and rubbed it on her hands and then on Ida's wavy hair. Mom combing her hair always soothed her.

"You know, angel, things are always going up and down. Life is exciting, then it's boring. People are nice, people are mean. One minute you feel like the happiest person on earth, and the next you feel like the loneliest. It's the same thing everywhere."

Ida bent her head into Mom's lap and burst into tears.

"Danya loves you very much, even if she doesn't know how to show it. Sisters love one another. They just do."

Mom paused, thinking about her own sister.

"Honestly, I don't think I could have grown up without Malayka. She was like a mother to me after our Mama and Baba died."

Mom gazed for a long moment out the bedroom window.

"Mom?" Ida blew her nose so she could hear better. "What happened to Aunt Malayka?"

Ida's mom paused.

"Car accident," she sighed. "But she shouldn't have died."

"What do you mean?" Ida asked.

She tried to push aside her own sadness, as an even deeper sadness seemed to wash over her mother.

"I don't want to burden you, angel."

"I want to know," Ida insisted.

Her mom moistened her hands with olive oil again and began rubbing Ida's back and shoulders.

"She was a journalist, you know. She'd go out into remote parts of the West Bank to talk with people and listen to their stories. About settlements releasing their sewage into Palestinian villages, and Palestinian farmers whose olive trees were uprooted in the middle of the night. Or being poor because Israel wouldn't give them a permit to cross the checkpoint so they could get to work. She'd put their stories on radio and TV so that others could hear them. Palestinians heard their stories. Jordanians heard them. Even Israelis did."

Mom stopped talking and Ida sat quietly, waiting...

"So, what happened?"

"You don't have to know all the details," Mom said.

Ida sat up, abruptly.

"Yes, I *do* have to know," Ida said, adamant. "I have a right to know. She was *my* aunt."

Mom pulled Ida into her lap.

"I suppose you're right, Ida. I can be too protective, because of things our family has been through. But if I keep shielding you from the truth, I stop you from staying true to who you are."

Ida played those words over in her head as her mother

started to comb Ida's hair again.

"Malayka was on her way to interview a Palestinian Bedouin family. It was a place called Ayn Qinya. I used to go there with her sometimes." Mom smiled as she remembered. "You can drive for an hour and never see another person, except maybe a sheepherder. That's actually a blessing because the roads are so narrow and winding and steep and broken that if there was a lot of traffic, there would be even more accidents than there already are."

"Ouch," Ida blurted out as the comb got caught in an unexpected knot.

She immediately regretted breaking Mom's train of thought.

"Is this too complicated? Boring?"

"No, Mom. Tell me, please. I have to know my own family, don't I?"

Mom nodded.

"Malayka must have swerved to miss something. Maybe a sheep or a goat. She went down a small embankment and her little car crumpled up. A piece of metal got lodged in her knee."

"That doesn't sound like something you'd die from," Ida broke in.

"You're right. It shouldn't have been. Malayka called our brother, Jubran, from her cell phone and although she seemed disoriented, she was able to tell him where she was. He was in Jordan, but he called the Palestinian Red Crescent in Ramallah, the nearest city. It should have reached her in half-an-hour. On the way, though, the ambulance got stopped at two Israeli military checkpoints. Both times, the soldiers searched the ambulance completely, taking everything out, dismantling plastic panels on the inside, opening the upholstery, interrogating the driver and the medic."

Mom paused again, but Ida could see she was too upset to keep talking. So, she waited patiently.

"It took the ambulance more than four hours to get to Malayka. She was still alive, they told us, but she didn't make it back to Ramallah. She had lost too much blood."

Ida gasped and Mom pulled her close for a long hug.

"I'm sorry you didn't know her," her mom said.

Ida almost confessed to her mom right then that she did know Aunt Malayka. Almost told her everything she'd learned in Busala. But she wasn't sure it was real, and she managed to keep quiet.

"You are very much like her, Ida. Caring about people. Fair to a fault, standing up for others. Malayka seemed to see it too, from when you were little, even though she never met you. That's why she sent you that pendant. She said you would be doing courageous things and you needed all the extra protection you could get."

"Protection?" Ida asked.

"The words from the *Quran* engraved on your pendant are special. They ward off evil. I'm sure she prayed on it too. That's a lot of protection for an eighth-grader, don't you think?"

Mom put the comb on the desk, smiled and left the room.

⁎⁎ ⁎

Ida got dressed, overwhelmed by feelings that she didn't understand. She looked out at the trees outside of her window—more plentiful and healthy looking than the trees that grew willy-nilly in the parched desert soil of Busala—and tried to think about what Mom had said.

"Aunt Malayka died because the ambulance was delayed by Israeli soldiers?" she said aloud.

Ida recalled Aunt Malayka's husky laugh. Her brown sugar perfume. The way she lifted Salwa with so much love it looked effortless. Fury overcame her. Then she thought about what Mom said about Ida caring for other people, standing up for them. Ida had absolutely no idea how mom could come to that conclusion about her. Ida was not a person to stick up for anybody—not even herself—and she *never* did dangerous things. Why would her mom think Ida was brave? And why would Aunt Malayka?

"Ida! Hurry up! Carolina and her brother are waiting downstairs to take you to the movies!"

Danya pounded on the door so ferociously that Ida was jolted out of her thoughts about Aunt Malayka.

"Okay, okay."

Ida pulled her poofy hair back into her signature loose ponytail, grabbed the purse that had her birthday money in it, and opened the door to leave.

"Wait!" Mom called.

"Ask Mario to take this *basbousa* to Carmen," she handed Ida a Tupperware full of the semolina and honey dessert that Carolina's mom loved.

"I'll take that down," Danya said, grabbing the Tupperware and rushing to the elevator before Ida even knew what happened.

Ida sighed. *My sister is so weird,* she thought.

⋆ ⋆

In fact, Carolina's brother left them at the entrance to the mall and sauntered toward the food court where the teenagers hung out. Mario was super nice, but he apparently had no intention of being seen inside the mall with his little sister and her friend. But almost immediately Carolina got a text on her phone and Ida saw that it was from Mario. It said: "Let me know if you need anything and I'll come right away."

The girls were happy they had a little time before the movie started and decided to see if there were any good sales on summer clothes. Holding Ida's arm (*just like the Palestinian girls do*, Ida thought), Carolina moved them quickly toward an accessories store where she always found cute things that were cheap.

"How are things over there at the good old Andrew Jackson?" Ida asked, caring a little more than she wished to admit.

"What do you expect from a school named for Andrew Jackson?"

"What do you mean?" Ida laughed.

"I never thought twice about the name of the school either. But my brother says it disrespects the history of Indigenous and Black people. And everybody."

Carolina was looking at herself in the mirror, holding earrings up to see how they looked.

"Isn't it just a name?" Ida asked.

"Mario says you can know a lot about a place from what they name their streets and schools. You can know what they're proud of and how they want other people to see them."

"I know what you mean," Ida responded. "In Jerusalem, the Israelis are changing the names of streets from Arabic to Hebrew. It's not enough that they take control of the actual street. They have to erase all traces of Palestinians too."

Only half-listening, Carolina held a purse with a fake cheetah design next to Ida's eyes to see if the color matched.

Usually, Ida loved having Carolina dress her up, but it seemed a rather stupid waste of time now. She looked at Carolina and at the few other customers in the store. As far as Ida could tell, no one seemed to know or care that on the other side of the world there were people—her people—risking their lives to save their homes from bulldozers and their families from arrest.

"Come on!" Carolina snapped her out of her daze, wrapping a fancy silk scarf around her neck and pushing her in front of a mirror.

Ida smiled at herself shyly while Carolina tried to smooth down Ida's hair as if she were grooming a magazine cover model.

But then Ida noticed in the reflection that the salesclerk was watching them, suspiciously. Ida froze.

Carolina immediately felt what was happening and

turned around.

"Is there a problem, ma'am?" she asked firmly.

Ida held her breath, fearing the woman would call store security or something.

"I'm just here to help you girls," the woman said, a little too sweetly. "Shall I ring that scarf up for you at the register?"

"I don't think so," Carolina replied, wagging her finger at the woman with the kind of teenage attitude she could never show at home.

Carolina pulled the scarf off Ida's neck draped it over a nearby rack, and pulled Ida toward the exit.

"We're not spending our money at a store that's not friendly to kids who look like us," Carolina called out over her shoulder loud enough for the other customers to hear.

How in the world did Carolina make it through that whole deal without swearing, Ida asked herself as they left.

The girls walked fast but in silence until they reached the food court at the far end of the mall. Carolina was still breathing fast and hard, and her mouth twitched like it wanted to shout. It was not the first time something like this had happened to her.

"Should we complain?" Ida asked, when she found her voice.

"To who?" Carolina replied. "You don't get anywhere by complaining. You've got to expose people like this, show everybody what they're doing."

"Oh."

Ida found Carolina's idea just as overwhelming as the incident.

⋆⋆ ⋆

The girls decided to change things up so they could enjoy the movie. They went to the homemade ice cream counter and looked at the white, pink, green, and brown flavors lined up in tubs, as if they didn't already know what they would order.

"Two scoops of vanilla chocolate chip with hot fudge, please," Carolina announced, and, without even checking to be sure what Ida wanted, she added, "Same thing for her."

"Extra hot fudge!" Ida said, with a pang of mischievousness that reminded her of the good old days, the days before she knew stuff. Knew where she came from. Knew where she could be now. Should be now.

The girls ate at a small round table near the window of the store so they could watch shoppers passing by. They talked about the women who wore those 5-inch heels and imagined where they might be going, but Ida wasn't fully concentrating on the conversation. She was having a separate conversation with herself in her head.

"This is the most delicious ice cream I've ever eaten. I could never, ever live in a place where I couldn't eat this ice cream whenever I wanted to."

"They don't have this ice cream in Palestine. The people in Busala won't ever get to taste it in their whole lives."

"I know. And two scoops cost more than dinner for a whole family in Palestine."

"I know. I'm going to throw it away right now."

"And what will that accomplish? If you throw away your ice cream, will they get to eat dinner?"

"I was selfish to buy it in the first place."

"That doesn't make sense. Just because they don't have nice things doesn't mean that you shouldn't have nice things. Does it?"

Ida's distress must have shown on her face because Carolina interrupted, almost on cue.

"Why do you always think so much? Let's just go to the movie, okay?"

★ ☆

They bought tickets for *Alice in Wonderland in 3D* and found perfect seats—in the middle, near the back of the cinema. Ida had read the story, of course, but the movie was even stranger than the book. She was already overflowing with the images and sounds of her own crazy life, and she couldn't handle the movie, which, like her life, didn't make any sense.

The Cat had just asked Alice, "How do you like the Queen?"

Alice, noticing that the Queen was listening, answered, "She's so likely to win, that it's hardly worth while finishing the game."

And right there in the cinema, Ida fell into a dreamless sleep with those cardboard and cellophane 3D glasses on and her jumbo popcorn tucked between her knees.

10

Upside Down

By the time Ida woke up on Sunday morning, the Oldbridge apartment was spotless, and the kitchen was shining. For the first time in her life, it really sank in for Ida that Mom did everything for the family. She cooked and cleaned and did the laundry and the shopping. Mom managed the school schedule and the doctors' appointments and so much more. Danya helped when asked, though she always did the minimum and complained while doing it. Ida often did little and hadn't even noticed it.

Ida slipped into the small kitchen next to Mom. Ida's hands moved quickly and confidently just like Mom's as they arranged food on small plates and warmed pita bread over the gas flame. It seemed so natural.

During breakfast, Ida watched Mom. Her eyes were bright and focused. She radiated an aura of contentment that she didn't have in Palestine. *Maybe she feels relieved not to have to worry that her husband might get arrested or her children might get tear-gassed on their way from school,* Ida thought. Dad, on the other hand, looked older. He was out of shape. Apparently, being a phys ed teacher at a school doesn't mean that you get enough exercise. But what upset Ida most was that Dad seemed far away. She was sitting right next to him, but she missed him so much it ached.

"Big day today," Dad said to Danya, as he refilled the plates in front of her with honey and *labneh,* a thicker and tarter version of yogurt. They were eating Danya's favorite breakfast.

"You guys don't have to come, you know." Danya was moody, as usual.

"And miss my baby's ballet solo?"

Mom jumped out of her seat to kiss Danya on the forehead.

"We're so proud of you. Don't you know that?"

Danya pushed her chair back and carried the empty plates to the sink without even answering. Dad looked angry. Danya wasn't being respectful. She looked like she wanted to get in trouble for some reason. Mom gave Dad a look that seemed to say, "She's under a lot of stress. Just let it go."

"Teenagers!" Salwa said with an exaggerated tone of exasperation, breaking the tension in the room.

Everyone laughed except Danya, who went to the bedroom and locked the door behind her.

At noon they piled into Dad's car. They dropped Danya

at the theater so she could dress and slick her frizzy hair into a bun and put on her only-for-dance-performances-and-never for-school make-up. Dad parked the car on a residential side street where he said the traffic cops never gave tickets. They had an hour before the theater doors would open to the audience, so they walked through the grounds of the community college, one of Salwa's favorite places.

"What do you think they're reading?" Salwa asked, pointing with her head to the students sprawled on the grass, some relishing the sun and some relishing the shade.

"I suppose they are reading philosophy or science or poetry," Mom answered, holding Salwa's hand and swinging it high.

"And some are just reading the newspaper," Dad added being practical.

"Let's go to the Art School. Please! Please! Please!" Salwa was jumping up and down and begging—not in an I'm-out-of-control way, but more like a please-let-me-learn way.

"We'll be late for Danya's performance, Salwa. We'll go another time."

"You should never miss a chance to make a child happy," Ida said, though it just popped out of her mouth, and she was as surprised as everyone else at her big-sister wisdom.

Mom conceded.

"We don't have much time, though. So, when I say it's time to go…"

"I'll leave right away without a fuss." Salwa finished Mom's sentence.

The lobby of the School of Art was impressive. The walls were covered with huge collages made of ripped up photographs with the spaces between them painted in—just waiting for someone to walk off the street to appreciate them. Last year when they'd come for Danya's ballet performance, the exhibit at the School of Art had been about patterns. Salwa had loved it, but it gave Ida a terrible headache being completely surrounded by dots and lines of bright colors. Now the exhibit in the main hall was about cities in Africa. There were too many words in the explanations next to the photographs as far as Ida was concerned, but the pictures were interesting. She noticed the dirt looked redder in Africa than it did in Palestine and the sun was a warmer color, not so harsh.

Despite her promise, Salwa couldn't help but complain when it was finally time to go. She could have stayed all day, reading and asking Dad what the big words meant. Ida saw Salwa as she had never seen her before. She could imagine Salwa walking these very halls with a clipboard, a crowd of students following behind her, writing her every word into their class notebooks. *There is so much opportunity in this country*. Ida bumped into a wall, turned bright red, and the image evaporated, but the idea of Salwa as a university professor had been solidly implanted in Ida's brain.

✦* ☆*

The family made their way to theater and tiptoed up the steps out of respect for its grand architecture, and the magnificent performances it had hosted. They took seats near the middle of the center section and sat, quietly breathing in the smell of the dark wood and cold brick. It was a regional show, hosting the top performers from ballet schools around Eastern Massachusetts. Mom greeted a woman a few rows in front of them. Her daughter was a dancer in Danya's old ballet school.

"Do you remember that woman's name?" Mom whispered to Ida, her eyes moving to the woman she had just greeted.

"No."

"Ayman?"

"I don't know these people, Somaya, that's your job."

"Mom," Salwa whispered, "her daughter's name is Gale. Danya hates her."

"Yes, you're right!" Mom smiled.

Mom made a note on a piece of paper and slipped it into her overfull purse. Then she looked up and smiled at the woman again, a bit too widely.

When the lights finally went down, Ida had trouble keeping her eyes open. Classical music always put her to sleep. According to the program, Danya's solo was the fourth number. When it was time, Ida sat up straight to see past the people sitting in front of her.

A faint spotlight shone in the center of the stage, and Danya walked gracefully through the dark and posed in the soft circle of light, exuding a calm, hopeful, beauty. Ida held her breath. Danya was stunning. Her hair, pulled into a bun, was highlighted with sparkles. Her deep blue eye shadow matched her blue tutu, and her pink rouge matched her immaculate pointe shoes. She looked like the fragile but perfect ceramic dancer on top of Carolina's mom's most precious music box.

In the silence she stood perfectly still, facing the right side of the stage. Her left leg pointed behind her. Her left arm crossed her body in front, and her right arm, held high, framed her face. She showed no awareness of the four hundred pairs of eyes trained upon her.

Suddenly, the energetic sound of violins erupted like school children let out for recess. Danya turned directly to the audience, a smile bursting across her face as if she couldn't contain herself. She jumped onto pointe and twirled toward the audience sweeping her arms in large circles as if to bring the audience into her embrace. Then, as light as the sound of the little metal triangle, she kicked and jumped and turned, in perfect time to the music, which was full of joy.

Then, there was a slow part and Danya looked heavy, as if she'd lost herself. She stretched and contracted as if she were sobbing and she ran in all directions before collapsing, unable to escape her sadness. But then the music softened as if the sun were rising. Danya found the strength within herself to go on and to celebrate life again. She danced and posed in all the corners of the stage, as if sowing seeds for the future. As the music rose to a crescendo, Danya leapt high and twirled over and over, and Ida felt a kind of homesickness as she remembered a time when she too had flown…

After the show, the family waited until Danya had changed and they watched her negotiate the crowd of people hanging around to greet the dancers. She thanked them politely as they went on and on about how beautiful and talented she was. When she reached the family, she was glowing and, for the first time—at least the first time in Oldbridge—Ida saw who Danya really was.

⋆⁎ ⋆⁎

Mom had prepared all the ingredients for *maqluba* the night before; she just had to layer them in the big pot. The dish was called "upside down" because it was assembled in layers and after cooking, the pot was turned over. First came the fried cauliflower and eggplant, then whole chickpeas. Mom threw in some diced carrots, though it wasn't traditional, because she said it made the dish healthier. She carefully laid down the chicken pieces, which had been boiled and then fried in "chicken spice" from the Armenian grocery store. She poured the washed rice on top and jiggled the pot back and forth so it would fill up the little crevices between the food. Mom measured the broth, to which she had added whole cardamom, ground cinnamon, freshly ground nutmeg, and an allspice mix called "*behar*," before heating the pot to a boil and turning it down to cook for an hour or so. Meanwhile, she whipped up lots of yummy salads. Red cabbage. White cabbage. Yellow and orange peppers. Avocado. Everything was bathed in fruity-peppery olive oil.

"Ida, *ya helwa*," Mom said. "Grab the olives from the kitchen. We're ready to eat."

Dad turned the pot over onto a big platter, and the family burst out with ohs, oohs and wows. The dish had come out perfectly, each layer laid out colorfully on top of the one beneath it. The table looked amazing, and everyone rushed to sit.

Ida set the dish of olives on the side of the table farthest from her. She felt scared of them and longed for them at the same time.

"Dad?" Ida asked, even before digging into the steaming food on her plate.

"Uh-huh?" he mumbled, his mouth full.

"Why did you guys leave Palestine?"

Dad nearly choked.

"Why are you asking that now?"

He sounded defensive, as if he'd been accused of a crime, but Ida somehow knew that under his armor of anger, Dad felt shame.

"Just wondering. I mean…I don't know, it must be hard for you to be away from your family all this time."

Ida looked at her parents. She realized her question had hit a nerve and she tried to soften it.

"Of course it is hard to be away from them. But you're our family too," Mom spoke up.

"You think it's better for us here, Dad?" Danya broke in, surprising everyone.

She wasn't challenging him, and the sincerity of her question seemed to catch Dad off guard.

Ida hadn't realized that Danya ever thought about Palestine.

Dad looked back and forth from Ida to Danya and then to Mom. Then he hung his head over his hands, clenched on the table.

Even Salwa seemed to be holding her breath waiting for Dad's answer.

"We didn't sit down and decide to raise our kids in here in the States," he began.

He was looking at mom as he spoke, as if he needed her support to tell a difficult story.

"It was the second *intifada*, the second time we rose up against the occupation, and the Israeli response was fierce. Palestine wasn't safe, especially for people our age."

Mom nodded, encouraging him to continue.

"When our education was interrupted, the whole family pitched in to send us here to study. Then I got a job teaching phys ed, and we decided to stay for a while so that Danya could learn English while she was small and experience things she wouldn't have the opportunity to do there."

As Dad spoke, his head was shaking as if he himself didn't understand why they had stayed so long and couldn't believe that he was raising his children outside of his homeland.

"When you were born, Ida, we just stayed. I had a decent job by then and our families kept telling us that it was too difficult at home. It just gets worse and worse over there. It's not the Palestine we wanted to give you."

"I understand," Ida said, noticing for the first time how sad Dad's eyes were.

"But your brothers stayed," Danya followed up. "And they have good lives, don't they?"

"Four of my brothers stayed." Dad said.

"And my brother and sister stayed," Mom said.

"But one of my brothers left and my two sisters left with their husbands. Many of my uncles and cousins have been forced to leave over the years. That's why you have relatives in Kuwait and Sweden and Jordan and Canada," Dad continued.

"It makes your grandfather angry, I think. But it's the Palestinian story," Dad sighed.

The girls didn't ask any more questions. The room was noticeably quiet, with only the occasional request for some-one to pass this or that plate of food. But mom kept laying her hand on each person's shoulder or head, randomly, to give comfort or to just make sure they were still there.

Ida chewed and her mind wandered to Busala. She thought about the sounds of gunfire at night and the anxiety of the teachers and students when armed forces came into the village. She thought about the lines of stress on Mama's face as she wondered whose home would be demolished next and when their turn would come. *Perhaps America is better,* Ida told herself. She said it a second time, hoping that it would make it true.

Ida snapped back to Oldbridge when Danya reached past her for the olives and, with uncharacteristic kindness, offered some to Ida. Frightened by the powerful magic in the olives, Ida shook her head and instead reached for more *maqluba*, the upside down, as she was hit by the irony of it all.

11
Shooting Randomly

The last few kids were dashing into Writing Social Science as the shrill bell announced the start of the period. It was a special class that students had to apply for by writing a composition, and it was open to eighth, ninth, and tenth graders. It was Ida's favorite class because there were only twelve kids instead of twenty-four, and the teacher, Ms. Williams, made it really fun. Ida was on guard, but so far, no one had treated her like they thought she was a terrorist.

"Today I'll return the assignments you submitted last week. They were good, so don't get upset if you see a lot of comments written in the margins. These are just ideas for you to consider if you want to improve your writing. All of you did really impressive work."

Ida smiled and looked to her left and right to catch someone's eye, and immediately remembered that at school she was safest when she was invisible.

"And we'll be starting a new assignment today," Ms. Williams continued, "one that will develop your writing, research, and cross-cultural skills." She paused and smiled. "And I think you'll find it really fun."

Ida's new assignment was to describe a day in the life of a girl her age living anywhere outside the United States. She would have to do independent research about the place and the conditions.

"And I know you'll like this," Ms. Williams said, getting excited talking about it, just like Ms. Bloom when she talked about the passion project. "I want you to get in touch with someone your age who is living in the place you've chosen. Use Facebook or any of your other sources to make a new friend to whom you can ask questions and test the accuracy of the research you've done. But remember to follow the internet safety rules I gave you."

"Only old people have Facebook, Ms. Williams," one kid said. "Can we use Instagram?"

"Ouch," Ms. Williams smiled.

"You can use anything you want, as long as you have your parents' or guardians' permission. Got it?"

Ida had to admit, it did sound fun.

"You don't have to write a separate paper. I just want to see you incorporate what you learn into our discussions in class."

Ms. Williams handed back Ida's previous assignment, and she was disappointed to find there was only one comment written on it. It was a poem, Ida's first ever. They had read a Greek myth and discussed it in class. Ida had really enjoyed the discussion, though she didn't participate because she was sure anything she said would sound stupid to the ninth and tenth graders. After the discussion in class, they had written poems with the title, "If I were Zeus…"

Ida had written her poem quickly, but it wasn't *that* bad, she said to herself.

> If I were Zeus
> And had the power
> To change the world
> In just one hour
> I'd not fight or wound or kill
> I'd just sit happily atop the hill
> They call Olympus but I call "home"
> And there I'd sit and never roam
> Cuz Zeus thinks he's God
> But is God so vain?
> Using power to hurt
> Is just insane
> If I were Zeus
> I'd use my powers
> To plant flowers.

In the margin, Ms. Williams had written: "You can plant flowers, now, Ida. You don't need to be Zeus."

Ida blushed in embarrassment, but luckily, no one noticed.

⁑ ⁎

The rest of the school day passed unremarkably, getting progressively more boring as the day went on. Ida realized that boredom was good. It meant that she wasn't holding all that fear. Kids might still be after her, might be planning to hurt her in some way, but Ida shrugged off any thought of them. Whatever happened wouldn't be as bad as having your home demolished. Ida could handle Oldbridge.

Last period was government and civics, and Mr. Nguyen wasn't giving his usual lecture.

"Who is going to summarize the chapters we read about migration?" Mr. Nguyen asked the class. "Daryl?" he asked right away, as if he knew no one would volunteer.

Daryl stood up as was expected in Mr. Nguyen's class.

"Um. Well. People moved around a lot."

He had longish blond hair and a southern accent that made some kids who thought they were geniuses think that Daryl wasn't too smart.

"Please give us a bit more detail, Daryl."

Ida felt for Daryl, and now it seemed like the other kids did too. There was an audible rustling of feet, as if they could feel what it was like to be in his shoes. Many of them hadn't read the chapters, either. And those who did couldn't remember them that well or didn't want to.

"Um. Well. People move around a lot," he paused, "from one place to another?" Daryl offered.

He was the tallest kid in the class and stood hunched over so he wouldn't stand out so much.

"I see," commented Mr. Nguyen. He seemed more hurt than angry. "What does 'migration' mean, Ida?" Daryl sat down.

Darn. Apparently, Ida wasn't invisible after all.

"Migration means moving around, but not like on vacation, but to live in another place for a while or forever," Ida said, already starting to sit down again.

"Good. And what are some reasons that people migrate to another place to live?"

Ida was on the spot. She tried to remember what she had read.

"Sometimes people move to find jobs because they can't earn enough money to live in the place where they were born?"

"Good. What else?"

Mr. Ngyuen seemed encouraged.

"And sometimes...they move to a new place," Ida said tentatively. "Because there are more opportunities. Like to get land to farm or find chances to go to school?"

"Excellent. Any other reasons?"

It seemed that Mr. Nguyen was looking for something specific, but Ida wasn't sure what it was.

She stood awkwardly for a minute thinking.

"Um..." she stalled.

She strained to remember the notes she had made from the chapters. She remembered using little green stars and underlining in pink. But she couldn't, for the life of her, remember the words she had highlighted. With the eyes of the whole class on her, she felt like the kids' hatred was beginning to close in on her, and she reached for an image that would make her feel safe.

Ida thought about Carolina. Her parents had come to the United States from El Salvador because of war there in the 1980s, and she had visited only once to meet her grandparents, aunts, uncles, and cousins. Then Ida thought about her own grandparents, aunts, uncles and cousins in Palestine and how war had torn their family apart. Then she remembered the strength and sadness in *Siddo's* voice when he spoke about the *Nakba*. Ida spoke with a confidence she didn't know she had.

"Mr. Nguyen, some people move because of war. They run away to protect their families, or they get chased away by people who want to hurt them or take their country."

A voice from the front row echoed Ida's.

"My family came to this country in the late 1800s...

It was Lizzie, the girl from homeroom. She stood up and turned to look at Ida as she spoke.

"They came here because it wasn't safe for Jews in their village of Slavuta in Eastern Europe. They needed to find a place where they could be who they are, without fear."

She nodded to Ida as she spoke, as if she agreed with what Ida had said. But Ida wondered what Lizzie's point was. Was she saying that her family's experience was worse than Ida's? Or that she understood Ida because of what her own family had been through?

"Yes girls! Thank you both. You may sit down," Mr. Nguyen said.

"Mr. Nguyen?" asked a kid who never said anything

and, as usual, didn't appear to have been following the conversation.

"Did you come here from China?"

"No, Brian. I'm from Vietnam," Mr. Nguyen answered patiently.

"Everyone, please open your textbooks to the world map on the inside cover and find China and find Vietnam. They're both in Asia, and they share a border, but they're two different countries with different histories, different languages, and different problems. Do you want to hear my story, about how I got to the United States, Brian?"

"Sure, I guess," Brian answered.

"Then we'll do that first thing next class. But before then, I want you to go to the world history and civics links that are on our class syllabus. Find out everything you can about Vietnam and the Vietnam War. Oh, and Daryl?"

"Yes sir?"

"I'll be calling on you first."

"Oh. Thanks for warning me."

The class laughed and even Mr. Nguyen smiled as the bell rang signaling the end of another school day.

☆ ☆

Tuesday was more of the same. Boring classes mixed in with not-so-boring classes. Ida wrote her assignments in her notebook, color-coded by class and the number of points each assignment was worth. At home, as usual, she started at the top of the list and finished each assignment, checking them off, before moving on to the next. Again, her eyes got stuck on the "Passion Project," now highlighted in yellow on her bulletin board and underlined with rainbow colors. Knots of fear spread from her stomach into her arms and legs making her feel weak. She had never before so completely ignored an assignment. What if she got up in front of the whole school and her parents and had nothing to say? Ida tried to dismiss her fears. *It's a silly little speech.*

Ida got permission from Mom to use her Facebook account to look for a kid she could interview and was surprised to find a page for Busala village (and Mom had already liked the page!). She posted a message asking if there was a girl who could help her with a school assignment. Then she figured that since she had permission to use the laptop, she should take advantage of the opportunity to play a game.

"Help! They're attacking my brain!" Ida spurted out, involuntarily.

Danya and Salwa ran over to the computer, sincerely concerned.

"Use a chomper," Danya spoke with urgency, "or one of the potato land mines."

"She can't. On this level, the zombies move too fast. See? Now they're pole vaulting."

Salwa was wise beyond her years.

"Put one of those tall nuts down!" Danya suggested.

"Too late for that too."

Salwa really knew what she was talking about.

"What should I do then? They're getting into the house."

Ida was hysterically firing with the peashooters, but the plants were clearly losing.

"Help! They're eating the plants! What should I do?

"Too late, Ida, you're dead," Salwa said unsympathetically. "You can't just wait around when the zombies are attacking your house."

Danya put her hand on Ida's shoulder.

"This is a really hard level, but you can win if you prepare yourself and have a plan. You gotta plant defenses. There's no other way."

Salwa and Danya wandered back to their homework. No need to stand there waiting for the inevitable. But Ida kept shooting randomly and muttering, "It isn't fair. It isn't fair. It isn't fair."

12
Layla

On Wednesday morning, Ida felt more than butterflies. Her arm muscles ached from gripping her stuffed animals too tightly all night. The idea of being home alone after school, not knowing what would happen, made her head spin.

"Mom?"

"Hurry up, Ida. We can talk later."

Mom was slicing pita bread in half at lightning speed. She had spread roasted eggplant, *babaganoush,* on one half with the back of a spoon so fast that her hands were a blur. The way she dropped in some chopped cucumbers and tomatoes, and put each sandwich in Tupperware with a sprig of red grapes, was mesmerizing.

"What have you been doing for the last half hour? Your bed isn't made, your hair isn't combed. Can you try to move a little faster on school mornings, *please?*"

This was the same lecture Ida heard every day and she was so used to it, she just waited for Mom to finish so she could ask her question.

"Okay, Mom, and I was wondering…"

"Don't wonder in the morning, Ida! Do your wondering in the afternoon when you come home. Today is your stay-alone day, so you'll have lots of time to wonder later. Now, you need to *move*."

"But that's what I want to talk to you about. Can I go to Carolina's house after school today and do my homework there? It's because, um, I have an assignment and I might need her help."

Mom stopped making sandwiches for a minute and looked at Ida.

"I don't mind as long as Mrs. Duarte is at home. Did Carolina ask permission from her mother to have you over?"

"Yes, it's fine with her," Ida lied. She never, ever lied (well, hardly ever), but this was really important.

"Okay then. Go to Carolina's, but please finish your homework while you're there."

She went back to making sandwiches.

It was strange for Mom to remind Ida to do her homework. She seemed to sense that Ida was no longer the perfect child she'd always seemed to be.

⁕ ⁕

Ida's school day was routine, but she was distracted. Everyone was buzzing about the passion project competition that would take place on Saturday afternoon. All her teachers would be there. All the parents would be there. They had even invited some officials from the city and Department of Education. The local newspaper was expected to interview the winners, who would each get prizes. Saturday was only three days away and the Monday school-wide presentations were just two days later, and Ida hadn't planned anything.

Ida was glad to go to Carolina's house after school. She was scared of going home alone, scared that the world would turn inside out again, scared that she might lose herself and never be found. Mrs. Duarte served Ida's favorite Salvadoran stuffed tortillas, *pupusas*, but with cheese, not pork, since she knew that Muslims weren't supposed to eat pork. Ida asked Carolina some questions about the kids in her old school but quickly realized that she didn't care how they were or if they missed her or felt badly about chasing her out of the group she'd grown up with. Ida was done.

The girls went into Carolina's room (which she didn't have to share with anyone, Ida noted for the ten millionth time) and lay down on the fluffy rainbow carpet. Carolina's room looked like a photo spread in *Teen Vogue*, but instead of choosing one matching color scheme, Carolina had mixed the colors up. The bedspread was yellow with green and blue pillows. The curtains were red, which should have clashed with the fluffy rainbow carpet, but somehow didn't. The bookshelves were pastel orange with black accents. Carolina's room looked like her—original, honest, and unconcerned with what anyone else thought.

The girls spread their books around them and, before long, they were finished with their math.

"Want to practice your speech on me?" Carolina asked, breaking the silence.

"No."

Ida didn't even look up when she answered.

"I guess I'm going to have to work more on mine," Carolina said shyly. "I got chosen!"

"To represent Jackson in the regional competition?"

"Yes!" Carolina grabbed Ida by the shoulders and they jumped in circles squealing.

"You're so going to win, Carolina! I'm so proud of you!"

"So, are you done with your homework?" Carolina asked when they had calmed down.

"I have something to do for my Writing Social Science class, but I need to use a computer. I'm supposed to talk to a girl my age who lives in another country."

"That sounds fun!" Carolina said, but Ida wasn't looking forward to it so much anymore.

"Come use my mom's work laptop," Carolina offered, opening it up on the kitchen table. "As long as you're using it for homework, she won't mind."

Ida logged into Facebook to see if anyone had answered the status she had posted. She had written a simple message, not expecting an answer.

> "I'm a Palestinian American girl looking for a girl from Busala who is around 14 years-old who can help me with a school assignment."

To Ida's surprise, there was a response!

> "I name Layla from Busala village. My English no good,
> sorry. Father show me your message. I help you?"

Ida immediately invited Layla to be her friend and Layla immediately accepted. Less than five minutes later, Ida found herself chatting with Layla, though she didn't have a clue about what to ask her.

> "Hi. My name is Ida."
>
> "I name Layla."
>
> "Isn't it kind of late there? I mean, most people are
> asleep at this hour, aren't they?"
>
> "Everyone sleep. I watch YouTube."
>
> "No school tomorrow?"
>
> "I no go school this week."
>
> "That is lucky!"
>
> "No. I miss friends. I lonely at home."
>
> "Why don't you go to school?"
>
> "I sick. Legs and hands hurt."
>
> "That's terrible."
>
> "Only have arthritis. Thank God not cancer."

Ida froze. *Arthritis? Layla?* She recalled the brief conversation at the girls' school in Busala.

Could this be the same girl?

Layla told Ida about going to the doctor. She told her about missing school. About losing her friends. They seemed to chat so easily.

"Ida, dear?"

Mrs. Duarte was standing next to Ida and sounded so loud.

"Are you sure you're doing homework? I don't want your mother to get angry with me for letting you play."

"No, Mrs. Duarte. I'm not playing. I'm chatting. I'm supposed to talk with someone my age from another part of the world."

"I'm doing that now, too, and I'm in eleventh grade," Mario interjected.

Carolina's brother almost never spoke to Ida, but he sat down across from her at the kitchen table to ask about her assignment.

Ida felt her heart jump into her throat.

Mario wasn't tall, and for that reason alone, he couldn't be called "cute." But he worked out at the gym, and his muscles were visible on his arms and legs. Mario had a few pimples, but it was easy to overlook them because of his very kind, dark brown eyes and spikey, rock-star haircut.

"You should keep in touch with that girl after the assignment," Mario advised. "I kept in touch with one of my friends in El Salvador and I'm going to be spending the summer with him."

"Really?" Ida was intrigued. "Isn't it dangerous there?"

From the corner of her eye, Ida saw Mrs. Duarte flinch, and she realized she'd hit a nerve.

"I'll be careful," he looked meaningfully at his mother. "And sometimes you can't not do scary things."

"What do you mean?" Ida asked.

"I mean, when people you care about need you, what are you supposed to do? Go to the movies and eat ice cream?"

Mario didn't realize the example he'd used hit so close to home with Ida, though he must have noticed the heat rise to her face in shame.

"You're very good hearted, Mario, and I admire that..." Mrs. Duarte started.

"But what?" Mario cut her off.

"*Amor mio...*"

Carolina's mom seemed to morph into another person when she spoke Spanish. Ida could imagine Mrs. Duarte holding Mario when he was born, swearing she'd do anything in her power to protect him.

"They tried to 'recruit' my brother as a fighter in the war! He was only ten years old! Why do you think we left everything we knew and loved?"

Mario and Carolina comforted their mother as if she were a child having a nightmare.

"Things change, Mama. They change when we change them."

The conversation felt familiar to Ida, but she still felt out of place. She excused herself from her conversation with Layla, signed off on Facebook, and put away her books. She moved slowly, not because she was distracted, but because some things were coming together in her mind.

"Mrs. Duarte, I'm going to head home now, okay?"

"I thought your mother was picking you up when she finishes work," Carolina cut in.

"Yeah, well her plans changed this morning and she

asked me to walk home," Ida lied again. She noticed that it was getting easier.

"Can't you wait until Armando comes home with the car so Mario can drive you?"

"Actually, Mrs. Duarte, there's something really important that I need to do at home. And it can't wait."

"What is it?" Carolina asked.

Ida's mind was already out the door and halfway home.

"I don't know yet," Ida muttered to herself under her breath as she left.

⋆⋆ ⋆

Ida walked briskly all the way home, sometimes jogging to move more quickly through the quiet neighborhood streets between Carolina's house and her apartment. She went up to the ninth floor and exhaled in relief when she realized she was alone.

She booted up Dad's laptop and opened Facebook, pleasantly surprised to find Layla still online.

> "Hi Layla. I just got home. Isn't it the middle of the night there?"

At first, Layla didn't answer so Ida thought that Layla had gone to sleep having left the computer on. But a few minutes later, she got an answer. The letters showed up very slowly, typed one at a time.

> "A-W-A-K-E"

Ida started to respond, but saw that Layla was still typing.

"…fingers hurt…"

A few minutes later, Ida got another message.

"Medicine too expensive. Quit school. Please visit?"

Ida felt like she'd been punched in the stomach. *She had to quit school! That's not fair!*

"Of course I want to visit you, Layla."

And after Ida typed it, she was surprised she really meant it. She then confessed, as much to herself as to Layla,

"But Palestine is very far from the United States.
I don't know when I can come. I don't know if I will
ever be able to come."

And that's when the phone rang.

"Hello?" Ida assumed it would be some company trying to sell her something. She hoped it was a computer so she didn't have to feel guilty hanging up on a person.

"This is Ms. Eva from Riverview School. Is Ida available?"

"Um, yes?" Ida's good phone manners had evaporated like water on the tarmac on a hot day in Busala.

"Is that you, Ida?" Ms. Bloom tried again.

"Ah."

Ida accidentally answered the way Palestinians do when they agree with something that's been said. In English it just sounded like a meaningless grunt.

"Well, I have good news for you, Ida," Ms. Bloom said, genuinely upbeat.

"Oh, thank you." Ida said, trying to regain her composure.

"You are one of our top five students at Riverview, and you have been chosen to represent our school at the regional passion project competition on Saturday!"

Time stopped.

Ida saw her hand drop and heard the phone land on the cradle. Her finger felt Aunt Malayka's pendant around her neck as she heard her footsteps on the way to the kitchen. Then, before she registered what was happening, the sharp taste of Aunt Malayka's magic olives exploded in her mouth. Ida didn't have time to decide if she was running *to* Palestine or running *away* from Oldbridge. But she knew that this was one of those situations in which she had no choice but to run.

13
Ashtrays in the Living Room

Ida squished some dough in her hands and tried to make the room stop spinning.

"So, what do you hear about the home demolitions?" Malayka asked Mama. All the women were working together in the kitchen.

Aunt Malayka had come over to help Mama and the girls make *ma'janaat*—little turnovers stuffed with spinach or cheese—that they would serve when a crowd of people came over that night, as they had every night since things started heating up in the village.

"You're the journalist, Malayka. You tell me."

Mama was chopping onions faster than those expensive vegetable slicers you see on TV.

"Where do you think I get my information? From my sister, of course."

"What would I know, being here in the house all day, cooking?"

Mama sounded like she was joking but there was bitterness in her voice.

"Stop complaining, Somaya. If you want to work, just go do it. Ayman isn't stopping you. The girls aren't stopping you. You studied journalism just like I did. I've told you a hundred times that I can help you get a job at my news station if you want."

Mama stopped chopping.

"You know I want to…and I don't want to at the same time. I want to be out there helping. But I'm not getting any younger, and Ayman would love to have a boy." Ida bristled at the thought of having a loud, stinky baby brother, but kept it to herself.

Mama turned toward the window, her eyes glazed over in thought.

"Then again," she continued, "I feel I already have more than a full-time job with the girls plus caring for Ayman's mother and father."

"That's work you do that helps everyone," Malayka said gratefully.

"I feel lucky to be here when the folks upstairs need me, especially since we were so young when our parents passed on. I'm upset because of the family. Honestly, I don't even know why I'm upset!"

Mama was picking up knives and putting them down and picking them up again like she was having a meltdown.

Malayka moved toward her and touched her cheek.

"Somaya, with all the talk of home demolitions, Israeli forces in the village, gunshots…how could anyone be sure they can keep their loved ones safe?"

"If things weren't so bad…so up in the air…" Mama said, her hand moving to her belly. "But who could bring another life into this world? We inflict too much on our children."

Mama crumpled into Malayka's strong arms like a ragdoll. Danya and Ida took up the chopping.

The women produced trays and trays of turnovers, baked in anxiety.

⁎⁎ ⁎

There wasn't a moment that entire day that Ida felt she could leave the house to visit Layla. But she did manage to phone her.

Layla was ecstatic to get a call from a friend. She said she was bored to death and that her mother wouldn't let her have any visitors.

"She thinks I'm going to break if someone touches me," Layla giggled, but then stopped abruptly.

Ida could hear the pain in her voice.

"If I stay still, I get stiff. When I finally move, it hurts bad. But if I move a lot, it hurts all the time," Layla explained.

Ida didn't know what to say.

⁎⁎ ⁎

After dinner, teenaged boys and young men started ringing the bell. Salwa buzzed them in, proud to have an important job to do. They made their way to the living room where

147

Baba had set up about twenty folding chairs he'd borrowed from neighbors. Basel was there, along with his friends Mohammed, Mohammed, and Hamoudi. Ida's cousins, Wissam and Taher, the sons of Mama and Aunt Malayka's brother, Jubran, had been released from detention earlier that day. They showed up with five or six other teens. There were eight or nine kids from Baba's soccer team at the boys' school. And there were a few girls, too.

One was an older girl named Mureen who was famous in the village for spending almost a year in jail for spray painting "Free Palestine!" on the walls of an Israeli restaurant. Ida knew she should show respect to this brave girl, but she was distracted by Mureen's huge front teeth, which made Ida wonder if she talked like a rabbit. Mureen brought a few girls with her, excitement steaming from them like when rain falls on a roadway in the summer. Ida realized that unlike in cities, this was an unusual scenario in Busala. The girls' parents probably didn't know they were at a meeting like this—crammed with men and boys—and that their reputation as "respectable girls" might be at risk.

Mama suspended her no-smoking-in-the-house rule and set ashtrays all around the living room. She put some bottles of Coke and Sprite, and a stack of plastic cups on the coffee table. Next to that, she put two heaping trays of *ma'janaat*. The yeasty smell of freshly baked bread was so strong and delicious that it almost overpowered the tangy odor of men who had worked all day in construction, or out in the fields.

⭐ ⭐

Wissam's loud voice cut through the buzzing of side conversations. Having just been arrested, he had some new credibility with the group, though he knew he could lose it if the Israelis managed to make people suspect he was a collaborator.

Danya had explained it to her. After someone was arrested, they were required to report to the police station every day. It didn't matter if they sat alone in an empty room or were interrogated. The fact that they went in and out made neighbors wonder if the person was giving information to the Israelis. Sometimes police even came to the house of a Palestinian and gave him money in front of a lot of people, as if it were a payoff for providing information. Everyone knew the Israelis did this, but collaborators were dangerous, and people were scared. Wissam and Taher acted extra tough to counter any doubt in people's minds. Being labeled a collaborator was like a death sentence in the village.

Wissam started what sounded like it might become a long speech.

"Brothers, there will be home demolitions again soon, and the Israelis will use all the brutal methods they can think of against us…"

"And we should be ready"—Baba interrupted, trying to steer back the conversation—"with a plan to protect our homes and families."

"Why wait, Uncle?" Wissam challenged him, but made sure to show respect to his Uncle Ayman, even though he

was disagreeing with him. "We should attack now, when they don't expect it."

He was playing to the crowd, but he clearly believed what he was saying.

Baba paused, as if deciding how to respond, and the room grew quiet. People seemed to expect a long debate.

"You're saying we should act first, not wait to react?"

There was surprise that Baba welcomed a point Wissam had made.

"Yeah," Taher jumped in, more loudly than necessary. "Let's get them before they get us."

Murmurs of agreement rose up around the room, and Ida felt jitters in her stomach. She had a brief urge to suggest karate. The soldiers probably couldn't defend themselves against karate. Then she realized how stupid that sounded and bit her lip so she wouldn't laugh out loud.

"So, what's the plan?"

Baba gestured for Wissam and Taher to pull their chairs around the coffee table. He took out a notebook and pen, and turned to a clean sheet. Then he looked up and observed the whole group, assembled together in the room. There was an uncomfortable silence, broken only by one of the boys from Baba's school sneezing.

Wissam spoke first.

"Let's collect weapons and store them in places around the village, like on the rooftops of the tallest buildings. We can see the occupation forces clearly when they enter the village, and quickly gather around our stocks."

Baba showed no reaction and simply wrote in the notebook.

"We can assign young *shabab* to each building where the weapons are stored. Everyone will know in advance what building they are supposed to go to when the soldiers come in. We can shoot down on them before they even know what's happening."

Wissam was smart and had thought it through. He seemed encouraged that his idea was gaining acceptance with so little resistance.

There was quiet while Baba wrote down Wissam's plan. Baba read over what he had written and looked up.

"Where do we get these weapons, *shabab*?" Baba asked. "How many of you have guns?"

This was a very unusual and possibly even dangerous question to ask in front of so many people. But Baba was trying to make a point.

The boys looked at one another. People knew that there were a few guns in the village. But they were owned by criminals, who cared only about themselves. They weren't likely to take the risk of letting their weapons be used against Israelis, unless they could make a lot of money from it.

"What about those guards up at the checkpoint at the entrance to the village?" Taher offered tentatively. "Maybe we could steal their guns?"

Mureen, the tall girl who'd been arrested, spoke up.

"Too dangerous. The guards who sit in the watchtower can see everything that's happening below. If we tried to steal guns, they would radio for backup, and more troops

would be there before we had time to get away."

Once a girl had spoken, other girls felt they could speak, too. Still, Ida and her sisters were surprised when the next voice they heard was Mama's.

"What if that's what they want us to do?" Mama asked simply from the hallway.

There wasn't even room for her to squeeze into the living room.

"What do you mean, Somaya?" Baba asked.

"The Israeli army likes when we attack them. Then they can shoot at us whenever they want and say it was in self-defense."

Wissam objected.

"So, we just sit here, Auntie Somaya, and wait for them to demolish our houses? And let Auntie Malayka put it on the news so the whole world can feel sorry for us?"

Wissam spoke louder to impress his father, Jubran, who had just come in.

"Haven't you seen enough of what their bulldozers do?"

The rest of the kids sensed the conversation was getting personal. They shifted in their seats and stretched to be able to see everyone who was talking.

"Look, *ya shabab*. These are two different issues we're talking about at the same time," Baba said, glancing at Jubran, appealing for some calm.

One of the boys sitting next to Baba got up to make room for Ida's uncle to sit, but Jubran remained standing in the hallway near the front door, poised to storm out in anger any moment.

"We agree that we want to be prepared," Baba continued. "Deciding if we want to act or react is one of the first decisions we have to make, and I think we're all in agreement that we want to take action. Am I right?"

He looked around at everyone in the room. Some nodded. But others were expressionless, as if they wanted to keep their options open.

"Whether or not we want to use arms is a different question."

Baba paused for a moment.

"Somaya, why are you against using weapons?"

Ida accidentally squealed. She felt proud that Baba was bringing Mama into the conversation.

"Don't waste our time, Ayman," Jubran boomed. "Of course, Somaya is against armed resistance. She doesn't want anyone to get hurt. Any mother would feel the same way."

How did Uncle Jubran manage to sound both insulting and respectful at the same time? Ida puzzled.

"Of course, I don't want anyone to get hurt," Mama replied.

She jostled her way into the room and stood across from her brother, where she could speak to him directly.

"You don't either. No parent wants their children to get killed. But you're wrong if you think that's why I'm against using arms. I'm not naïve, Jubran. Our people are going to get hurt either way, whether we use weapons or not."

"So, what's your point?"

Jubran seemed to want Mama to hurry up so they could

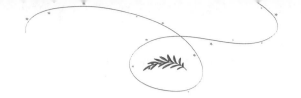

focus on what he thought was the reason for the meeting—planning an attack.

"Self-defense is our right," Mama continued. But they have more weapons, more soldiers. Violence is a losing strategy for us. We need more people to stand on our side. There are other ways to resist that are more powerful."

Ida had never seen Mama so forceful. Danya and Salwa also shined with pride.

Even Jubran seemed a bit caught off guard, as the kids in the room pondered Mama's words.

But some were not convinced.

"We might lose. Fine," said Basel. "But at least we don't let them get away without paying a price."

Ida couldn't keep quiet any longer.

"So, we know we're going to lose, and we know people will get hurt or killed, but we keep going with this strategy anyway? Can't we think of anything better?"

Baba, Mama, Danya and Salwa turned in shock with their mouths hanging open. But Aunt Malayka smiled as if she wasn't at all surprised.

"My controversial niece!" she whispered to Ida.

Ida was surprised her Aunt Malayka actually believed that being controversial was good!

Just then, the *adhan*, the call for the nighttime *'isha* prayer, rang out from the mosque on the east side of the village, followed a few seconds later by the slightly softer call to prayer from the mosque farther away on the west side. The men stood up to pray, and out of the corner of her eye, Ida thought she glimpsed the man who had come to her house in Oldbridge with Aunt Malayka's olives. Her heart skipped a beat thinking that he might recognize her. But before she got a good look, Ida was caught in the wave of women who were being guided by Somaya into the next room, where she handed out towels, since there weren't enough prayer mats.

⁎⁎ ⁎⁎

After they had finished praying, everyone regrouped in the living room. Ida studied every face, but couldn't see the man who had brought the olives and figured he had slipped out.

"Let's think about this," Baba said.

He wanted to get back to what Ida had said before they broke to pray.

"They have more weapons than we do. Their strength is force. What are *our* strengths?"

It was an odd question. No one rushed to answer.

"We're fearless. They're cowards," Jubran insisted. "We have justice on our side and they..."

"That's what I mean," Baba interrupted. "We have strengths that they don't. We can use our strengths the way we choose to and increase our chances of winning."

No one had any idea what Baba was talking about. He sounded like a university professor or something.

"What if..." Ida ventured. "What if more people knew what was going on here. I mean, *really* knew who we are? So many people have been fooled into believing we're a bunch of hateful terrorists."

"Why don't we invite them here?" Mureen jumped in.

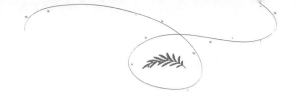

The angry scowl that had seemed etched on her face relaxed into a look of cautious hope.

"Who?" Baba asked.

"Let's call that young Israeli guy, Uri—the one who always comes here with a group to stand with us when we have demonstrations. Maybe he can bring some Israelis and foreigners to stay with us, in our houses, to see what happens here."

An unsettling silence spread through the room.

"*Shabab*. And *sabaya*," Baba said with a respectful nod at the girls. "We can think of many ways to win that are in line with our values, like Mureen's idea. Let's meet again tomorrow to see if we can agree. It's late now, and I'm concerned that your parents will not be pleased."

⁎ ⁎

The living room slowly cleared, with only Jubran, Wissam, and Taher staying behind. Mama and Malayka had already reverted to their usual roles, picking up overflowing ashtrays and throwing away plastic cups. Salwa had long ago fallen asleep on the couch. Ida swept up crumbs in the hallway just out of sight of the living room. Clearly, the meeting wasn't over, and she didn't want to miss anything.

Uncle Jubran was still standing there.

"I don't know what you're trying to do," Jubran warned Ayman.

"It's no secret, Jubran," Baba replied. "I'm trying to avoid making the same mistakes we've made in the past. For years. Decades! So many people dead, in jail or pushed out, and we just keep using the same losing tactics to give them our sons' lives and our homes."

Jubran paused for a moment, choosing his words carefully, knowing he wouldn't be able to retreat from them later.

"When there's a threat, Ayman, you can't run away! You have to stand up for the village!"

"There are many ways to stand up!" Baba insisted.

"You think we're weak! Israelis come to walk on you, and you lie down and say *'itfaddal.'* Welcome!" Jubran shouted.

"They come to shoot you and you say *'itfaddal,'*" Baba blasted back.

⋆⋆ ⋆

Aunt Malayka took advantage of the lull to bring Salwa a before-bed drink. It looked like regular water in a glass, but Aunt Malayka said it was a "Fear Cup"—water that had been left under the stars to absorb the power to eliminate fear. Mama said it was a stupid superstition, but as Malayka tucked Salwa into bed, Ida snuck to the kitchen to drink the last drops of the magic water from the glass.

"My boys won't be here tomorrow night," Jubran snapped as he left with Wissam and Taher.

The two had clearly come without permission. They would not be making the same mistake again.

14
Holding On to What's Left

"Thanks for coming with me," Malayka said as she leaned over to open the passenger-side door to let Ida in.

All day Ida had been looking forward to the time when Aunt Malayka would pick her up from school so they could go together to West Jerusalem, "the Jewish side."

"I would go anywhere with you, Auntie," Ida answered, climbing into the dusty, dented, little, red Fiat that Malayka was so proud of.

They waved to Danya and Salwa who were walking home, looking slightly jealous.

Aunt Malayka smiled.

"No one likes going to the doctor, but it's not so bad knowing that you and I will be able to stop into our favorite pastry store for some girl time."

The car wound its way up the steep main road that led out of the village. There were places where two cars couldn't pass, either because the road was too narrow or, more often, because some inconsiderate person had left their car in the middle of the street to buy something in a shop or chat with a friend. Too often, two cars would nearly crash, one driver jumping out of the car cursing and shaking his fists at the other, only to realize it was his cousin or his uncle. Then the two men would embrace and laugh, making the line of cars behind them wait even longer. Ida found it even funnier than the Egyptian comedies they watched before bed.

"Auntie?" Ida spoke up. "Can I ask you a question?"

"Of course, you can ask me a question, silly."

"Um." Ida wasn't sure she wanted to know the answer. "Why do you have to go to the doctor? Are you sick, Auntie?"

Before Malayka could answer, they reached the checkpoint at the entrance to the village, and instead of ignoring them as they often did, the guard motioned for the car to stop on the side of the road.

"Don't be scared, Ida," Malayka said, trying not to sound tense. "The guards will just ask questions and look at my identity card, and then we'll go."

"Step out of the car," a guard instructed, leaning over to inspect the car through the driver's side window.

His eyebrows were raised in an expression of boredom mixed with superiority.

"The girl too," he ordered, motioning toward Ida with his gun.

Ida and Malayka stood near the car while the guard took Malayka's identity card to another guard minding the checkpoint, who was a woman. They each looked at the identity card briefly, but then one of them put it down on a big boulder while the two continued to talk and sometimes laugh. Although she didn't understand Hebrew, Ida was pretty sure they weren't talking about Malayka. It seemed like they were talking about a party they'd been at.

After about five minutes, which seemed like an hour to Ida, the female guard gave Malayka her identity card and motioned for them to leave. They had not searched the car nor run the identity number through a computer. They had only delayed them and made them angry.

"*Imshi!*" the female guard shouted at Ida in Arabic, telling her to go when she didn't move fast enough.

The guard spoke in a harsh tone, and Malayka stiffened.

"There's no need to talk to her that way," Malayka hissed.

The other guard sensed the escalation and came over to find out what was going on.

"I'll speak to her any way I like," the female guard replied.

Both guards were taller than Aunt Malayka who seemed, for a second, to hesitate.

"Don't you have a little sister or brother?" Ida heard herself ask the guards. "Would you want anyone to speak to them the way you spoke to me?"

Ida turned and walked to the car without waiting for an answer.

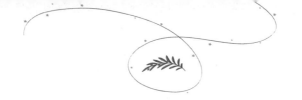

Aunt Malayka drove away, fuming in silence. As they pulled onto the well-paved road out of the village, an Israeli car coming from the settlement sped past them honking. Already angry, Malayka slammed on her horn as if to shout back, "I have just as much right to be here as you do if not more!" but the horn got stuck and wouldn't turn off. Malayka pulled to the side of the road and banged on the horn over and over to get it to turn off, but it wouldn't stop blaring. Both she and Ida scrunched down in their seats laughing with embarrassment, until finally Malayka got the idea to turn the car off, which also turned off the horn.

The car had a mind of its own, just like the people in it.

※ ☆

At the big intersection just a few minutes past the check-point, Ida already felt like she was in another country. Nothing—not the wide streets with sidewalks, the tall buildings with parking lots, the new cars or strangely dressed people—looked like it did in Busala.

Aunt Malayka put her hand solidly on Ida's knee and squeezed. It tickled.

"I'm not sick, Ida."

She was either pretending that nothing had happened at the checkpoint, or maybe there was just nothing to say about it.

"I have to go to this Jewish doctor to check on how my leg is healing. He's the best orthopedic specialist in town."

Then she added, almost as an afterthought, "You know, I might not even have my leg if it weren't for your mama."

Ida badly wanted to know how Malayka had lived through the accident. And how had Mama helped?

Malayka seemed to read Ida's mind.

"Do you remember when I had that car accident last winter?"

Ida nodded, anxious to hear the rest of the story.

"Your mama and I had gone to *Ayn Qinya* to see a family we care about. They had their sheep and goats stolen by Israeli settlers. I wanted to do an interview for the radio station, and your mama was doing the sound for me, holding the microphone and all that. Before we even got to *Ayn Qinya*, I had to swerve to miss a wild pig that had wandered onto the road. It was a narrow road and we went down a small embankment. My knee was hurt in the accident, but your mom took care of me. She wrapped her headscarf around my leg and the bleeding nearly stopped, which was good because it took the ambulance almost four hours to reach us."

Ida was silent for a long time.

"You didn't know that?" Aunt Malayka asked.

Ida shook her head…

After the doctor's appointment, Malayka and Ida walked to a pastry store. Jewish pastries were a thousand times more delicious than Palestinian pastries, Ida's cousins always said. Ida chose one mushroom and one potato for lunch and an apple pastry for dessert. She knew Mama liked her to have real food before sweets. Malayka ordered one chocolate pastry and a cup of coffee. She ordered in Hebrew and paid before they sat down near the window

where they could watch people in the street.

West Jerusalem felt so alive. Everyone seemed to be going somewhere. The shops were bustling. The sidewalks were full, some people wearing the latest boots and jackets, just like in Oldbridge. Others looked like they'd jumped out of a history book. Men dressed in the old-fashioned clothes that religious Jews wore in Europe, and women wearing long skirts with wigs, and lots of kids trailing behind.

A woman carrying a baby in a sling came to their table to ask for some sugar. Ida could understand "sugar" because it was the same in Arabic, but she didn't know how to respond to the woman. She hesitated and said in English, "Take as much as you want" and slid the sugar container toward her. The woman thanked her in English, took several packets, and went back to her table. Malayka looked amused.

"Why are you so tense, Ida? They're just people."

"I know they're just people, but they make me nervous. Now that I spoke to them in English, will they figure out that we're Palestinian? Will they attack us?"

Ida motioned with her eyes to a small table crowded with five fully camouflaged soldiers, men and women, with their machine guns lying casually on the floor under their chairs. One of the women soldiers was eating the same kind of apple pastry that Ida was eating.

"They might shoot at us in our village. Maybe even those same soldiers. But they won't shoot us here."

Ida looked confused.

"See that young woman making coffee behind the counter?" Malayka asked.

Ida nodded.

"She's Palestinian.

Ida raised her eyebrows.

"And see that couple in the corner holding hands?"

Ida nodded again.

"They are Palestinian too. They probably came here because it's unlikely that someone they know will see them and tell their parents. They could never act like that on our side of town."

"I don't get it." Ida admitted. "You mean the soldiers come to our village and arrest us and demolish our houses and then we come here and pretend that we don't mind?"

"Oh, we're not that shallow," Malayka looked amused. "It's complicated."

She paused to put her thoughts into words.

"They have stuff over here on the Jewish side that we want—pastry shops, malls, books, cinemas. Every person wants nice things. We want to enjoy our lives, right? And don't we deserve nice things as much as they do?"

Ida nodded. Aunt Malayka was really convincing.

"I come here when I want something we don't have on the Arab side—like the best orthopedic specialist in town. Just because I go to an Israeli doctor and eat Israeli pastries doesn't mean I give them permission to shoot me, does it?"

"I guess not," Ida said, but she still had doubts.

"You know that I went to an Israeli university?" Malayka continued. "I could have gone to one in the West Bank. Bir

Zeit University, An-Najah, Bethlehem University—they're all very good. But I wanted to be able to work in Israel. Why shouldn't I? It's my country, isn't it?"

"But you were so angry at those guards at the checkpoint."

"I was angry! I'm still angry, not just about rude soldiers, but about our whole situation. They continue to demand to be here not as equals, but as people with more rights than we have, just because they are Jewish. I am both angry and sad that it has gone on for so long, and that as hard as we work to change it, it often feels like things only get worse."

"Isn't that a good reason to stop dealing with them? I mean, if they aren't open to changing or even to listening to us?" Ida mused.

"Some of us boycott Israel, just like South Africa was boycotted, and that's putting a lot of pressure on Israel to change. The boycott, divestment and sanctions movement is one of our strongest nonviolent tools. But in the Jerusalem area, our situation is different. They took over Jerusalem, so we don't have a choice but to interact with Jewish Israelis all the time. We need to be able to talk to them, know how they think. The Palestinians outside are changing how our story is told, and we're here, holding onto the land, refusing to be erased from history."

"But the problem is too big, Auntie. How can anyone make a difference?" Ida complained.

"Look at you, Ida! You spoke up to those guards at the checkpoint. You made them listen. Because of you, they may think differently about what they're doing."

Ida thought about what her aunt had said. She thought about her Jewish friends in Oldbridge. Many of them had turned against her for no reason, but some seemed to go out of their way to be nice. She thought about how much she loved the apple pastry. Then she thought about the guards at the checkpoint. And the home demolitions. It was very confusing.

Ida and Malayka walked to the car without talking. Ida could tell that it hurt Aunt Malayka to walk uphill, so she moved slowly.

"Auntie?" Ida asked when they reached the car.

"Yes, *habibti?*"

"I was just wondering, what is an orthopedic specialist? You said yours was the best one in town."

Malayka laughed. "They work on bones and joints. Why?"

"Can they cure arthritis?" Ida asked hopefully.

"I don't know if there is a cure for arthritis. But orthopedic specialists help treat it. Why are you asking about arthritis, Ida?"

"My friend has it. Layla. She can't even go to school anymore. It's like her life is over."

"Layla, the butcher's daughter? The one in your class?"

Ida nodded, willing away the tears that came from nowhere like a sudden summer thunderstorm.

"I don't know what we can do, Ida. I know she doesn't have health insurance because her father is from the West Bank, and West Bankers don't have access to Israeli health care. He's been trying to get a Jerusalem identity card, like

his wife. But it's been years and years, and they've gotten no answer from the Interior Ministry. I doubt they have enough money to pay privately for treatment for a chronic condition like arthritis."

"But that's not fair!" Ida blurted, realizing she sounded childish.

"No, it isn't fair. Not one bit."

Then Malayka got an idea.

"Maybe I can talk to my doctor, the one who's taking care of my knee. He's a decent person. Maybe he'll treat her for free."

Ida threw her arms around Aunt Malayka with gratitude.

"You think he will?"

"I don't know. There are all kinds of Israelis. just like there are all kinds of Palestinians. Some of them hate us. Some of them don't like us but think we should be treated fairly. There are even Israeli Jews who fight alongside us for our rights. But sadly, there aren't enough of them yet to really change the way things are. At least not yet."

⁺₊ ⁺☆

Before going home to Busala, Malayka and Ida stopped on Salah Al-din Street, the main commercial street in East Jerusalem, as dusk fell over the city. The day vendors were selling their wares cheaply so they could go home lighter. The night folk were just venturing out full of energy. After spending the day feeling like a stranger in West Jerusalem, Ida realized she felt a deep sense of belonging among

Palestinians, as if she were made from the same stones in the street that Jesus and other prophets had walked on thousands of years before.

Ida watched as an old man sauntered nonchalantly down the sidewalk, suddenly noticing another old man sitting on a plastic stool and playing cards on an upturned cardboard box. The two men shouted greetings, embraced and kissed one another on both cheeks as Palestinian men do, as if they hadn't seen one another in ages. Ida knew, though, that this was a daily ritual. Friends and neighbors connected with one another. Even the repetitive greetings and questions about one's health and family were sincere expressions of caring among a people who had lost so much and were trying to hold on to what's left.

15
Running

The Friday morning quiet of the village intruded on Ida's sleep. She was vaguely aware of her sisters' rhythmic breathing; it lulled her back into a half-sleep and a strange dream took over.

In the dream, Ida saw herself again at Danya's ballet performance, but it wasn't at the community college, it was at the White House in Washington, DC. Aunt Malayka was sitting behind Ida even though the seat next to her was empty. The music started, and there were sounds of jumping and sliding, but the stage was too dark to see anything. When the performance was over, the audience clapped until their palms were bruised and bleeding. Then, the president came out to congratulate Danya, who was animated like a cartoon! He told Danya to make a wish and he promised it would come true. But Danya didn't want the wish. She put it

into a brown lunch bag and gave it to Ida so she could make a wish. All the people in the theater stopped talking to listen to what Ida's wish would be. Mr. Nguyen, Carolina's brother, Mario, and the girls from her school in Busala were all there, and so was the Israeli lady who had asked for sugar packets at the pastry shop. Ida opened her mouth to speak, but it got locked like that, wide open. The people around her acted as if that were normal and gathered their things to go home.

Ida woke up abruptly.

A pigeon had landed on the sill outside the window making a kind of purring sound. Ida wondered what the bird was trying to tell her. Farther away she could hear the tweeting of the little brown birds that fluttered everywhere in search of crumbs. There was also the caw-caw sound of the larger birds that seemed to be passing messages among themselves, just like the girls in school. Ida wondered if any of the birds' messages were for her. If only she could understand.

Later than usual, Ida and her sisters got out of bed and started the routine of cleaning the house, but their hearts weren't in it. At the meeting the night before, the village seemed to splinter into a thousand pieces. Basel and his friends had decided to collect stones on the rooftops of buildings around the village so they could throw them at Israelis who came into the village. This led to an argument between Basel and Danya, who, like Mama, thought that would get more people killed.

Mureen, without any support from anyone, had organized with Uri to invite some Europeans to stay with her in her mother's house and the homes of her cousins. Baba had contacted a lawyer to start a court case to stop the demolitions or at least delay them. But the lawyer told him it would take years and cost thousands of Jordanian dinars, which he didn't have. Doing her part, Malayka had gotten ten old video cameras from her news agency and was showing the older kids how to use them to document things like attacks by soldiers or other bad things that might happen. Ida had no idea what was right. She just felt sick about it all.

After the cleaning was done, Ida's parents and grandparents went together to an *'aza*, a memorial service for *Siddo's* older brother who had died that morning after suffering from lung cancer for two years. The women and men gathered separately to mourn, but children weren't expected to go.

Danya and Salwa were happy to have some unexpected free time. They wanted to go down to the small plot of land that *Siddo* kept in the backyard. Salwa enjoyed climbing the olive trees. Danya did too, but she was too old to climb trees without the neighbors gossiping about her. They liked to make themselves a picnic out of whatever fruits or vegetables were ripe on *Siddo's* trees and plants.

"Go without me," Ida said. "I don't feel well."

But when the door slammed closed and she was alone, Ida felt awash with sadness. She had never felt so lost.

Why, why, why did I come to Busala? There is nothing I can do here. Ida complained to herself.

Suddenly, the sound of whistling in the distance caught her attention. Whistling was the warning sound villagers

used to announce the arrival of Israeli forces. Within seconds, whistling seemed to erupt all around. Ida ran to the balcony to see what was going on. From her vantage point above the soccer field, she could see hundreds of boys gathering on the field. They were looking around, listening to the whistles and whistling themselves. On the roof of the school, she saw men with guns appear, too many to count. Ida felt her body tense the way it did when the music in a movie warns you that something bad is about to happen. She wanted to shout, to warn the boys about the men with guns on the roof of the school, or to press pause on the remote so the action would stop long enough for her to think.

But real life moves too fast.

Before she even caught her breath, Ida heard a loud bang. Then two more in quick succession. Tear gas rose up from the field. The boys scattered. They leapt behind boulders and sprinted into the spaces between houses to get away. It seemed only seconds until the field was empty, though the sounds of shouting in Arabic and Hebrew continued to fill the air.

Ida was paralyzed with fear. Her eyes scanned the scene, and she noticed a small blue and green lump on the field on the side farthest from her. She strained to see what it was, and her heart sank. It was a boy! A small boy had been on the field when the shooting started, and there he lay, unmoving, and no one seemed to notice, except her.

Without thinking, Ida bolted down the stairs wearing only her cloth house slippers, without even pausing to take the key to the building. She flew across the now-empty street, and onto the field. Ida looked up to the rooftops as she ran, and she saw Israeli forces, still pointing their guns toward the field, while their comrades chased *shabab* down the village alleyways. Instinctively, Ida raised her arm toward the shooters, perhaps to shield herself from the bullets she knew might come, or perhaps to signal for them to hold their fire.

It felt like an hour until she had crossed the field and reached the child. Her eyes stung and her throat burned with a bad taste from the tear gas. Ida wasn't strong, but she had no choice but to lift the boy over her shoulder and carry him off the field between two huge boulders.

It was Faris—Basel's little brother, the one who ate cheese puffs on the way to school!

He was soaking wet, but Ida was relieved to see that it wasn't blood. Too scared to run, he had fallen flat on the ground in place, and he had wet his pants.

"Listen to me, Faris," Ida said urgently.

Faris's eyes welled up and Ida realized that he might start to wail. She mustered all her patience and spoke in one of those fake, sugary voices that little kids love.

"No need to cry, brave Faris!"

Ida's eyes shot left and right trying to scope out her location and options. With a huge smile that didn't match the desperation in her voice, she said, "You and I are going to have a great adventure, Faris. But you have to be very, very quiet or your mama won't let you play. Can you do that?"

Faris nodded and stifled his sobs. Ida sensed that this irritating, badly behaved boy somehow understood that he now had to obey.

"Okay then. Follow me!" she whispered with as much upbeat excitement as she could muster.

Ida literally pulled Faris along the edge of the field through the small space between the line of rocks that marked the property lines of the neighboring buildings. It wasn't safe enough for her to make it back across the field to her own house, and certainly not with a little boy in tow. But she could make it to her uncle's house. No matter the differences of opinion between her father and Uncle Jubran, she knew without question that she'd be safe there.

Ida and Faris entered the alley. It was just wide enough for three or four people to walk side by side. She heard yelling in Arabic and Hebrew and wanted to keep going. But Faris was already tired, so they flattened themselves against a wall to catch their breath. Ida reached up to rub her stinging, tearing eyes, but little Faris pushed her hand away, shaking his head like he knew from experience that touching her eyes would make the pain even worse.

Seconds later, Ida heard the pounding of heavy military boots in the alleyway in front of them and realized they couldn't stop. She grabbed Faris's hand and pulled him forward toward the sound, ducking into a doorway just before a wave of green camouflage barreled by, walkie-talkies screeching. She and Faris hid under some unfinished concrete stairs that led to an unfinished second floor and slid behind an old washing machine that was stored there.

For the first time since she'd run out of her house, Ida had a second to think. She remembered that Danya and Salwa had gone downstairs to play outside on *Siddo's* land. She prayed that her sisters had made it back inside. She thought about her parents and grandparents at the memorial service. *There must be hundreds of old people there. They can't run. What will they do?* Ida worried.

"Happy birthday to you! Happy birthday to you!" sung by Alvin and the Chipmunks rang out from Ida's pocket, nearly giving her a heart attack. She had forgotten about the cell phone that her parents had given to her "just in case." She frantically pushed buttons so the ringing would stop before the soldiers found her and Faris. Then, she quickly set the ringer on silent and hastily sent a text message to her mother: "I am with Basel's brother, Faris. He is fine. Am trying to take him home. Don't call me because the soldiers will hear the ring." It wasn't a smartphone, so it took her forever to push the numbers to type such a long message. She noticed the battery was already low and turned the cell phone off.

* *

The soldiers kept coming and coming. It seemed like hundreds of them. Ida looked down at Faris to remind him to be quiet, but she didn't need to. He was so paralyzed with fear, he couldn't have uttered a sound if he wanted to. She felt bad for the little guy. Ida noticed a stinky yellow pool forming under him and soaking through her cloth slippers, but she didn't dare move.

When she could no longer hear boots, Ida knew they had to move quickly. Her uncle's house was only two doors down. She held her breath as they slid against the wall toward the entry. Ida was scared but forced herself to look in both directions. This alley was usually bustling—children playing, workers rushing home to eat, and students running to the market to pick up groceries for their mothers—but, because of the danger, there wasn't a person to be seen. All of a sudden, the sound of an approaching helicopter made the space feel small and exposed. Ida tried to calm down by imagining herself in her uncle's kitchen where, surely, her cousins were gathered, waiting, safe and sound, for things to return to normal.

At the entrance that led up to Jubran's building, the sound of her aunt screaming hit her ears before her brain could register what she saw. A soldier was holding Yamen, one of her little cousins, by the shoulder while her aunt was begging him not to hurt the boy. The soldier paid as much attention to her as you would to a used tissue in your pocket. He was busy talking to another soldier who was motioning toward the upper floors. The second soldier bounded up the stairs, presumably to look for more people in the building, and the first soldier pushed Yamen backwards into the house as the rest of the children shouted and cried. The officer walked in after them and shut the door.

Ida's vision blurred with tears as she turned abruptly and ran, Faris tripping behind her. The armed patrols hadn't seen them, but they had to get out of sight. But where could they go? She realized now that Israeli forces were occupying the buildings. Danya had told her that they did that during sieges. First, they took over one of the bottom apartments and moved all the other families in the building to that apartment. Forty, fifty, or sixty people could be crammed into one apartment, with one armed person to keep them in line, while another one or two went to the roof to watch for people running away. People like Ida and Faris.

Ida held Faris's hand as they ran toward the center of the village, away from Ida's house, but a little closer to Faris's. It looked like a ghost town.

Ida thought, *Where did everyone go?*

The shop owners had hastily slammed shut the heavy metal security doors to protect their shops, but some of the outdoor displays of handbags and plastic containers piled in big pyramids were still out.

Could the shop owners be hiding inside? Ida wondered.

Ida bent down to let Faris climb up on her back so they could move more quickly. The coldness of his wet pants made her shiver, but she focused on getting to a safe place. Except there was no cover out there. The street was wide, and the shops were attached to one another in one long row. There was no space to duck into or anything to get under.

They kept moving, Ida's heart pounding so loudly, she feared the soldiers might hear it. About ten shops down, Ida found a shop with an olive tree in a small courtyard behind a locked gate. It was Abu Mahmoud's store. Like the other one-man grocery stores in Busala, he carried just about everything except fruit and vegetables. He had baking

supplies, cleaning chemicals, canned goods and snacks. He also had batteries and glue and phone cards. Ida wanted so badly to stand under that tree, to feel the protection of its smooth leaves. She paused and leaned longingly against the gate, and magically, it swung open. From inside the courtyard, Ida could see that the heavy metal doors of the shop were slightly ajar, but the security bars were locked.

Ida ached to get in. It would be dark and quiet inside, and they would be able to rest. She closed her eyes to think, and her hand went to her neck where she found the engraved pendant. She stroked it, feeling next to it the three keys that hung from the same piece of yellow yarn. *The smallest is for the elevator in my Oldbridge building and the largest is for the door to our Oldbridge apartment. What's the middle-sized key for?* Ida asked herself.

Ida turned the middle-sized key in the lock of the shop's security bars, and they slid open with a soft creak. She and Faris entered the dark store and stood quietly to be sure no one was there. Ida noticed a small spiral staircase at the rear of the store and called softly to see if anyone was there, but there was no answer. She and Faris climbed the stairs and found the most cramped but immaculately clean room she had ever seen. The ceiling was low so she had to move around bent over. There were two mattresses on the floor of the room, one of which was behind a cheap screen with a tacky fake Indian design. There was a small set of drawers with piles of clothes folded neatly on top. They stood there for a few minutes, Ida praying that they were really alone.

"Go to the bathroom, Faris," Ida said gently motioning toward the toilet that was only partially hidden by a half wall. Faris went obediently, still without speaking a word. Ida sat down on one of the mattresses on the floor, and felt a wave of tiredness roll over her. It seemed as if every muscle in her neck, back, and legs had been straining. Faris came and sat close to her. She looked at him and felt a mix of irritation and concern. *Stupid boy! Why didn't he run like everyone else when the Israelis started shooting?* Then she felt guilty and patted his knee. He looked so small and helpless.

Ida took out her cell phone, turned it on, and quickly texted: "Troops are in Uncle Jubran's house. We are safe in Abu Mahmoud's store in the center." She sent the message and turned the cell phone off. If only she had a charger. Carefully, Ida approached the window and slid it open so she could hear what was happening in the village. It was eerie. There was almost no sound at all. The occasional gunshot, though far away, made both Ida and Faris stiffen. When this happened, she tried to remember to whisper to Faris, "What an adventure!"

Ida carefully went through the clothes in and on the dresser until she found a drawer of little girl's things, probably Abu Mahmoud's granddaughter's clothes. She found a pair of jeans that didn't look too girly and called Faris to put them on. He hadn't complained once about wearing wet pants, but the smell was really gross, there was dirt caked over the wet spots, and she knew he must be freezing. She also put her cloth slippers in the trash and took some socks and a pair of plastic shoes. They were much too big.

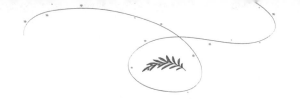

The pair made their way back down the spiral stairs to the shop to look for something to eat, Faris now clinging to Ida like she was his mother. Ida was both touched and irritated. She gave him some fresh yogurt from the refrigerator case, which he promptly spilled like white teardrops across the display of cereal boxes. She found him some bread and cheese and had some herself. They drank apple juice, a treat that Ida rarely had. She took ten shekels from her jeans pocket and put it on the counter next to the cash register.

The sudden rumble of jeeps coming down the street felt like an earthquake in Ida's chest. There was a slower, heavier sound too. *Could it be a tank?* she thought.

The Israeli authorities were shouting from bullhorns. They were speaking in Arabic, but the sound wasn't clear, and she couldn't understand them. Then there were sounds of men's and women's voices laughing. Ida guessed there were at least twenty of them. She pushed Faris into a cupboard behind the cash register and climbed in after him.

Ida was right to be worried. A moment later, troops swarmed the store having seen the gate open. Ida and Faris held one another tightly as the sound of boots got closer to the cupboard where they were hiding. They banged their heads against one another by accident, and Ida thanked God that Faris didn't cry out.

They heard someone open the refrigerator and the fizz of soda bottles opening. They heard the soldiers pop open bags of chips and throw them around to one another. There was a lot of talking, but Ida couldn't make out any of the words.

Running

Now I see what Aunt Malayka meant—It is better if we learn to understand them, Ida realized.

Outside, a jeep horn honked obnoxiously, calling the patrols back to work. The kids waited, absolutely still. Just when Ida was sure they had all left, a few of them returned. On all sides, things began to fall and break. She heard them kick in the refrigerator, spraying glass across the floor. One took a broomstick or piece of wood and banged the cash register near the cupboard where Ida and Faris were hiding. The destruction was fast and loud, and Ida nearly fainted from the horrible sound of it.

After the soldiers had left, Ida and Faris stayed in the cupboard for several minutes. Faris sobbed softly and held the skin of Ida's neck for comfort. When they crawled out, they saw a mess worse than they'd ever seen in their lives. Everything was broken, even the shelves and counters themselves. Dented cans were everywhere. Notebooks were mixed up with laundry detergent and pita bread. Burlap bags of rice and flour had been stabbed, scattering kernels across the floor. The plastic milk containers in the refrigerator cases were toppled, and the white liquid dripped from the doors.

Ida was overcome with guilt. "I'm so sorry, Uncle," she kept repeating. She knew Abu Mahmoud couldn't afford these losses. No one in Busala could.

Ida walked slowly to the front of the store and peered up and down the street. Just then, she heard the distant sound of sirens getting closer and closer. Ida grabbed a bag of bright orange cheese puffs that had been spared, pulled Faris onto her back, and ran.

16

Battle for Belonging

It was getting dark and a little cold, but Israeli armed forces were still in control of Busala, and Ida and Faris couldn't get across town to their homes. Neither could they safely stay still.

They moved silently, clinging to the outside of each building, looking down the streets and up to the rooftops before moving across the open spaces to the next building where they could take some cover. Abu Mahmoud's big house shoes made Ida slip and trip, so she left them behind and continued on in socks, looking out for glass, in addition to soldiers. They were moving in a wide circle, staying far from the soccer field but moving toward Faris's house near the girls' school from the far side.

Where are all the people? Ida wondered.

It was almost completely silent in the village, except for the now faraway sounds of the occasional helicopter.

When she heard the voices of children in the building next to them, her heart almost jumped out of her body with excitement.

Ida pulled herself up on the metal security bars under the window and called out softly. "Auntie. Please help us."

A few small faces peered down through the bars and smiled in recognition. But then a thundering voice shouted.

"Get away from the window!"

The words were in Arabic, but with a Hebrew accent.

A woman's arm reached through the bars just long enough to gesture for Ida to get away immediately.

Ida and Faris moved passed two more buildings, but then it suddenly occurred to her that Faris's house might be occupied too, and she couldn't hold it together anymore. Ida slid down against the building and pulled Faris onto her lap.

"Faris?" she whispered. "You are a very brave knight..."

Faris nodded without any expression.

"You know that's what Faris means, don't you? Your name means 'brave knight.'"

Faris smiled. His eyes shone with pride.

"But your leader doesn't know where to go. It's getting dark and we can't get to your house tonight. I'm so sorry."

Ida clung tightly to Faris, and tears rolled down her cheeks. She didn't even try to hide them.

"You know what your name means, Ida?" Faris spoke for the first time, and he sounded all grown up.

"I…" Ida stammered, trying to collect her thoughts.

"'Ida' means 'returning,'" Faris said. "It means that Palestinians always come back here. Your name means that you always get back to where you're supposed to be."

Faris waited while Ida wiped her tears on her jacket sleeve, and then he pulled her arm until she stood up.

"What is it, my knight?"

Ida let Faris pull her around the corner of the building where they'd just come from and into a doorway.

Ida gasped, disbelieving.

She stepped out for a minute and looked up to check her suspicion. There was the minaret, silent through the *'asr* afternoon prayer and the *maghrib* sunset prayer because no one had been able to reach the mosque to start the screechy, tape-recorded call to prayer. Faris had brought Ida to the mosque!

"You're an angel," she told him. "An angel!" and she touched her silver pendant as gratitude washed over her.

Ida and her sisters used to go to the mosque west of Oldbridge to take Arabic lessons when they were little. But Ida had never been in a mosque in Palestine before. Baba sometimes prayed in the mosque on their side of Busala. But women usually didn't go, and girls never did. She wasn't sure what she'd find in the mosque, but she had to move quickly to find out before the sunlight was completely gone. She could not risk turning on the electricity after dark and attracting the attention of the Israeli patrols.

Moving fast, Ida slipped around the big, empty room to lower the dusty curtains above the small windows that lined the walls. That blocked out the little light that was left so Ida couldn't even see Faris, who she had left sitting quietly next to the door. On her hands and knees, Ida

crawled across the worn carpet toward Faris and felt for the small, electric heater she had seen in the corner of the room. She plugged it in and it gave the room a spooky, dim glow. Ida couldn't leave that light on all night without attracting attention, but she did keep it on long enough to locate an old mattress and some blankets. She also found some bottles of water, which both of them gulped down thirstily, even though the water was warm.

Ida left the bathroom door open and memorized the distance to it from the mattress. She unplugged the heater and pulled Faris toward her, covering them both with blankets that soon got warm from their body heat. It could not have been past seven o'clock, but Faris was asleep right away. "Good job, brave knight," she whispered.

Ida was relieved that she wasn't alone.

Just before sleep overtook her, she remembered that her parents would be worried. She turned on the phone just long enough to send a brief message.

"In the mosque near the town center with Faris. Have water and blankets. Don't worry."

★⋆ ⋆★

Despite her exhaustion, Ida didn't sleep well. Faris's hair smelled like socks, and he held onto her neck so she couldn't move away. Even worse, her head was spinning with confusion about things that didn't make sense.

In Palestine, Salwa was irritating and whiny, but she fit perfectly in Ida's arms when they slept together on cold nights. Danya was always there for Ida, no matter what, but somehow seemed unsatisfied. She tried to think about her life in Oldbridge, too, but the images were starting to fade and blur. She saw Dad in her mind, yelling at her to pick up her room, but she couldn't hear the way he pronounced it "bick up your room." She remembered her school from the outside but couldn't imagine the face of her school bus driver. She pictured Carolina clearly but couldn't recall why it was so fun to hang out with her. Ida's memories seemed not her own, but like something she had seen on TV or read in a book.

✲ ✲

Ida must have dozed off, because the sound of gunshots woke her up. It was very dark in the mosque, and she had no idea what time it was. She moved Faris, still sleeping deeply, to the side and stood up. Her shoulders, back and legs ached. Her arms, hands and feet ached. Even her face ached. And she felt weak with hunger.

Carefully, Ida climbed the narrow metal spiral staircase that led up to the minaret so she could see what was going on. As she climbed, a diffuse, early dawn light flooded in—bright, but not yet hot. She strained to hear the comforting sound of roosters, but she heard nothing that sounded alive. The stairs ended on the open balcony at the top of the minaret, but Ida was scared of standing up straight, afraid of being seen and shot, but even more afraid of what she might see.

Ida mustered the courage to peer over the balcony railing and saw Busala, her village, spread out beneath her

like a grand welcome mat. There were still no cars or people in the streets. It looked flat and static like a painted canvas in a museum.

From this height, Ida could see the girls' school and, just next to it, temptingly close, was the six-storey building where Faris lived. On a normal day, she could have walked there in five minutes. She inhaled deeply and wondered how long it would take today.

In the distance, in the direction of her house, Ida could see what looked like smoke. It wasn't the black smoke that spiraled up when boys burned tires during protest demonstrations, and it wasn't the billowing smoke that choked the sky when stupid people burned trash in metal dumpsters. It was, Ida realized, not smoke at all. It was dust. It looked like the cloud of dust that escaped from the pillows when the girls cleaned the upholstery on Fridays—but much denser.

Ida couldn't take the time to think about things that didn't lie in her path. She looked again at Faris's building and planned a course through the village to get there. She would rather have stayed in the mosque until the Israeli patrols were gone, but there was no food. Her stomach ached and her head throbbed worse than on the first day of Ramadan when she wasn't yet used to fasting. And she was lonely.

She climbed down the stairs and heard Faris crying on the mattress.

"Don't be scared, brave knight. It's me, your leader!" Ida reassured him, trying to make her voice sound confident and happy, but she nearly laughed out loud at how ridiculous she sounded.

"I just went up the minaret to see what's going on. I didn't think you'd wake up while I was gone."

"That's okay. I knew you'd come back," Faris said, sniffling.

It was only the second time Faris had spoken since their ordeal started, Ida reflected. In fact, it was, the second time she ever heard Faris speak at all. Before all this, she'd only heard him whine.

Ida raised some of the curtains to let light into the dark room. She sat down next to Faris. The day hadn't started but she was already tired.

"You must be hungry," Ida said sympathetically.

"Very!"

"Can you wait here while I look around and see if I can find anything for us to eat?"

Faris shook his head and jumped to his feet.

"I'll come with you."

In the small office of the mosque, which looked like it hadn't been cleaned since the place was built, Ida didn't find any food, but she did find an electric teapot, tea bags, and sugar. She made two cups of tea, putting four heaping teaspoons of sugar in each. They drank their tea slowly and thought about what to do next.

"You know," Ida said, "we're not far from your house."

"I know."

"But I don't know how easy it will be to get there. I don't know where the soldiers are, or if they've already left the village."

Faris looked sad but listened attentively.

"It might take some time, and we still have to be careful and quiet while we're moving. Do you think you can do that?"

Faris pulled himself together and stood up to signal that he was ready to go.

"How about stopping in the bathroom before we leave?" Ida suggested.

Faris nodded.

⋆⋆ ⋆⋆

It took nearly an hour for Ida and Faris to navigate past the seven or eight buildings that stood between the mosque and Faris's house. The air was hot and still. Much of the time, Faris was too weak to walk, and so he rode on Ida's back. Ida had to rest frequently.

They crossed an open lot on their hands and knees, moving slowly to avoid attracting attention and stopping often to rest behind big boulders. Ida got a cut on her knee from a piece of glass and a gash on her middle toe that slowed her down. On her way across the lot, she had encountered a mouse, which nearly made her scream, and a snake that, luckily, was more interested in the mouse than in Ida and Faris. So early in the season, it was probably a harmless snake, but the reminder that they weren't safe made Ida long for home, any home.

They finally reached a spot directly facing Faris's building. Ida held him so he wouldn't run across the street before she figured out a plan. It would take only a few seconds to reach the front door. But what if no one was home?

Or worse, what if everyone was home and soldiers were occupying the building?

Ida hesitated.

Taking a risk, she pulled out her cell phone, but instead of sending a message, she phoned her mother.

"Ida, *habibti*, where are you? Are you okay?" her mother sounded hysterical with worry.

"We are across from the front door of Faris's building," Ida said softly. "But I don't know if I can cross. What if there are troops in the building?"

A short shriek came from Faris's building and almost immediately, the front door flew open. It was Ida's mother, with Faris's mother and Danya and Basel and Salwa and Baba and Faris's other brothers and sisters crowding behind.

Before Ida could speak, Faris bolted across the street and into his mother's arms. Ida instinctively glanced left and right and dashed across, too. The door slammed behind them, and a roar of cheers stung her ears after the long quiet. She was hugged and patted and carried up the stairs like a hero, though all she wanted was to be held in her parents' arms and to feel safe.

They plopped Ida and Faris down on the couch in the living room, and one by one, each person greeted and kissed her, congratulated her, and asked questions that she didn't know how to answer. It seemed like a long time before the noise level went down enough for Ida to say something.

"Why is everyone here?"

She still couldn't figure out what was going on.

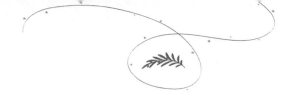

"We came here to wait for you," Ida's father said, his eyes watering with relief and pride.

"You're a hero!" Salwa chirped in.

"What are you talking about?"

Someone handed Ida a steaming bowl of rice with meat. She took the bowl, her hand shaking from hunger.

The people crowding the living room moved aside and made a space so Ida and Faris could see the television, which had been on the whole time, but with the volume turned down low. Ida's mouth fell open as she saw pictures of herself running across the field toward Faris. Pictures of herself plastered against buildings pulling Faris behind her. Pictures of herself carrying Faris on her back moving toward the mosque. On the bottom half of the screen, Ida saw the text messages she had sent, in quotes,. The TV journalist was talking about Ida, "…a fourteen-year-old girl who braved the dangers of a siege on her village to rescue a neighbor's boy."

Ida was speechless.

As the pictures and commentary played over and over again, Ida's family tried to explain, but it was a lot to take in at one time. Uri, the Israeli guy, had brought other young people to Busala, and they had taken videos of the violence from spots around the village. It was a coincidence that they caught Ida on tape running across the field. They uploaded film clips to YouTube and Malayka forwarded the links and the text messages to journalists she knew. Once it got on TV, Uri's people made a point of trying to film Ida with their powerful zoom lenses as she crossed the village. One of them, a South African man, had even been wounded by a rubber bullet, dangerous enough to kill, that grazed his shoulder. The shooter later said he thought the camera was a gun. Malayka sent the text messages in as they came, and the story became news.

Ida opened her mouth, but the words got stuck in her throat, and all of a sudden, she was crying uncontrollably. It hit her how close she and Faris had come to being hurt, that she might never have seen her family—either of her families—again.

But it also sank in that people who'd never heard of Busala, and maybe didn't care at all about Palestinians, now knew about the Israeli armed forces, the siege, and the home demolitions.

Ida realized that she wasn't invisible anymore.

17

Rubble

The Israeli forces were gone. The siege had ended. Villagers could move freely again.

Ida thanked Faris's mother for her hospitality. Faris's mother thanked Ida for saving her son's life.

Ida crouched down to give Faris a hug. He had been scrubbed clean and was wearing fresh clothes. He munched happily on cheese puffs, the crumbs sticking on his shirt making Ida well up with love. Maybe having a little brother wouldn't be that bad.

She could begin to imagine that her life deserved to have a purpose, that she could actually have a real passion project—like helping her people.

⋆⋆ ⋆⋆

Ida's family got into the car for the short ride home. It

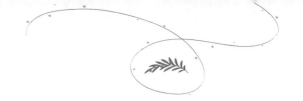

waddled slowly down the road as it hit bumps and holes that had been gouged by the military vehicles. Ida held her mother's hand tightly but kept her eyes fixed on the scenery. The village didn't look warm and safe as it had two days ago, but neither did it look as scary and empty as it had yesterday. It looked like a survivor of a disaster, stunned and battered, but still standing steadfast.

Just a block before they reached home, Ida caught sight of her friend, Layla, sitting on a big flat rock by the side of the road. She was wrapped in a blanket next to a huge mess of rubble that had been her home. Layla's father, mother, and a couple of neighbors, were sifting through the debris, putting items in bags. The roadside was littered with assorted pieces of furniture the police had removed from the house after breaking the door down. The washing machine and stove, bought new, sat on the rocky ground, looking battered.

"Baba!" Ida choked.

"I'm so sorry, Ida…"

"What happened?"

Ida was still in shock, but both Danya and Salwa knew what happened. They were crying. Mama looked like she was using all her energy to hold back her tears, too.

"As we feared, the bulldozers came and demolished their building. Layla's family was the only one living there. The other two floors had been rented out but no one had moved in yet."

The car was still moving slowly, but Ida jumped out and ran to Layla. Layla didn't acknowledge that Ida was there, and she wasn't reacting to the pile of broken memories in front of her. A bootlegged Zendaya CD, smashed in two. A pot of cooked wheat *freekeh* spilled onto the rocks. A lace bra. Layla's school backpack.

Baba saw that it was useless trying to get Ida back into the car, so her family fanned out over the wreckage and worked alongside Layla's parents trying to recover whatever small items of value might still be salvageable. No one spoke. There was nothing to say.

Layla's family had been in Hebron for a week celebrating her cousin's engagement. By the time they got home, the police, border guards, special units, municipal authorities and dogs had left. There was nothing they could have done anyway. The Israelis wanted to make a point to the villagers that no one was safe. Ida filled up with feelings of powerlessness and rage.

How could anybody destroy a family's home? Why does this happen, over and over again? Doesn't anyone care?

Ida turned toward the sound of crunching gravel and saw Uncle Jubran approaching with Wissam and Taher. Uncle Jubran reached Ida first and gave her a long, strong hug. Wissam and Taher waited their turn, each one saying they were glad she was okay. The three men climbed onto the rocks that had once been Layla's home and continued to sort. It obviously wasn't their first time.

Malayka drove up in her little red car and got out carrying a video camera, a long microphone, and a tape recorder. She gave Ida a big hug, but she didn't smile.

"*Ilhamdulilah assalamah*, Ida," Aunt Malayka welcomed

her home. "I'm so very proud."

Malayka took a deep breath and gazed at the rubble.

"Layla's your friend, right?" she said, distracted.

Ida nodded.

Malayka turned and put a firm hand on Ida's shoulder.

"I will always look after her for you."

Then, abruptly, she went about her work.

"Somaya, give me a hand?" Malayka called to Ida's mother.

Mama looked like a professional as she swung the tape recorder over her shoulder and held the microphone so that Malayka could set up the tripod. Before she pressed the record button, Aunt Malayka expressed her sympathy to Layla's father, and embraced Layla's mother as she sobbed, before pulling herself together.

Aunt Malayka stood in front of the camera with the microphone, while Mama expertly managed the tape deck and panned the camera from Malayka across the mess of concrete, to Layla sitting on the rock, still in shock. Malayka did the first piece in English for an international TV outlet, and then she and Mama used the sound equipment to interview the family in Arabic for local radio.

"After all that arguing, meeting, and planning, we lost," Ida said to herself, but loud enough for her father and uncle to hear. She felt let down by the adults. She had trusted them, and they'd failed.

"No, *habibti*. We haven't lost," her father assured her.

"How can you say we didn't lose?" Ida was angry. "Layla and her brothers and sisters have nowhere to live!

And Baba, she's sick!"

"Ida, we don't win or lose with one house. Of course, every house matters. Every family matters. But we will win in the long run, even if we suffer until then."

Uncle Jubran stood next to her father.

It started to rain, although there were no clouds, and both men glanced up to the sky and, simultaneously whispered *Ilhamdulilah*, thanking God for his grace.

★★ ☆★

Ida said goodbye to Layla, who barely looked up. Then she took Salwa by one hand and Danya by the other, and the sisters walked home together. There was nothing Ida could do here, but she now realized there was something she could do, that she must do.

Spotting their building, Ida was relieved and grateful to see it still standing.

As soon as they got inside, Ida sat Salwa in front of Baba's computer and opened a browser window. She took Salwa's face in her hands and looked deeply into her beautiful, familiar eyes.

"You, my little sister, are much smarter than you know. If you love me, you'll look at this."

Ida set the browser on the homepage of the Art School at the community college near Oldbridge. At first, Salwa looked confused, but then she clicked on the gallery exhibits, and was immediately entranced.

"And when you get bored," Ida continued, "you can play this."

Ida opened a new tab to Plants vs. Zombies. Salwa squealed with excitement.

"Maybe I shouldn't have done that," Ida admitted under her breath.

Meanwhile, Danya was waiting for her. They walked into the living room together and sat on the couch, as Ida fiddled with the remote control. If Danya wondered what Ida was doing, she didn't ask. She sat quietly, as if in awe, as if treasuring every moment with her, as Ida searched station by station up the hundreds of satellite channels

"Finally!" she announced, finding one about arts and culture.

It was a beautiful Russian production of the ballet "Sleeping Beauty" by Tchaikovsky. Princess Aurora was awakening from her deep sleep. The king and queen, the workers in the palace, and the subjects of the kingdom were all waking up and seeing one another and themselves with new eyes, seeing the world for what it really is.

Danya was mesmerized, and Ida thought she saw her sit taller, stretching her neck gracefully.

Feeling the pressure of time, Ida moved silently but briskly to the kitchen cupboard as if on a mission. She took out a container of green olives and put it on the counter as she took one last, loving look out the window past the balcony over the field.

Then she ate.

18
"Goooooooal!"

"Ida, move!"

Mom sounded angry.

Ida exhaled and looked around. Her family's apartment in Oldbridge seemed exactly the same, but totally different. Ida shivered as she imagined her home demolished by a bulldozer, losing all the special stuff she'd collected, and having nowhere to go.

"You're going to be late for your passion project thing!"

Mom was really losing her temper now. Ida noticed the entire family waiting for her by the door, shoes on, purses in hand, all ready to go.

"Don't worry. I'm home," Ida reassured her.

She went over to her parents and kissed them both, totally dissolving her mother's anger. Then she kissed each of her sisters. Salwa said, "Eew," and Danya gave her a strange look.

"*Yalla*, let's go," Ida said, smiling as she walked past them into the hallway and toward the elevator.

It had been a long day, but she didn't feel tired, or scared.

⋆ ⋆

Ida watched the passion project competition from the front row of the auditorium where the presenters waited until they were called for their turn. One by one, the eighth graders who had been chosen to represent the various public and private middle schools in the region talked about themselves, their interests, their hopes.

When it was Carolina's turn to represent Andrew Jackson Middle, Carolina flashed a smile at Ida as she walked up to the stage. She knew her friend would do well, but Ida's stomach was flip-flopping all over the place.

She need not have worried. Carolina's presentation was amazing!

She had taken photos of the customers who came into her parents' restaurant. She must have been doing this for a while because there were a ton of pictures. Some were of little babies. Some were of business people. Some were of teenagers. The people were Black and white and Indigenous and Sikh and punk and goth and in wheelchairs and all kinds of families. They were smiling and serious and shy looking. The pictures were bold and vivid and colorful and made you want to hug all those people, those beautiful people, like they were all your own big family. Carolina had timed each picture to change on the beat of the song "We are the World"—not the tacky new version, but the original one by Michael Jackson.

At the end of the song, Carolina came on stage from the side and stood right in the middle of the stage and snapped a picture of the audience, and they went wild, clapping and shouting. It was one of the happiest moments that Ida could remember in her entire life.

⋆⋆ ⋆

A few speeches later it was Ida's turn. Her stomach flipped over again, but then she pulled the yarn string with Aunt Malayka's pendant out of her shirt and walked onto the stage feeling strong.

She hadn't written down a single word, but Ida knew what she wanted to say. It felt a little strange standing in front of all those people. So she walked to the edge of the stage and sat down. Then she scooted over to the middle, to be sure she could see, and be seen by, everyone.

The auditorium felt very still.

⋆⋆ ⋆

"My family is from a village called Busala, right near Jerusalem. In Palestine.

It used to be a farming village. For years and years, families in Busala worked together caring for the land, the orchards and fields, the goats and sheep, right alongside their Jewish neighbors.

Then settlers came.

But not to live side by side with the people who were already there since forever. They took the land of our families and ancestors. Palestinians resisted, but many were kicked out or ran away from the war, and others were crammed into tents and buildings.

It's just like what happened to Indigenous peoples here. How they were pushed off the land and survived so much violence, as if they aren't even human.

In Palestine they're still taking our land, our water, saying where we can and cannot go, and demolishing our houses using bulldozers.

That's what happened to my Palestinian friend, Layla. Her family's home in Busala was bulldozed. Layla's a girl our age!"

Ida looked over at the kids in her class, the kids she'd tried all year to avoid.

"What would you do if a bulldozer was coming to demolish your family's home?

Would you beg them to stop?

Scream for help?

Run away?

Or might you pick up a stone and throw it at the bulldozer?

If you did throw one, would that make you a bad person?

Kids mostly know what's fair and what's not. What would you do?…

My Aunt Malayka never forgot what's fair. She used to go out all over the West Bank and listen to people who couldn't find work or were being attacked by settlers or who had no water or who'd been arrested for demonstrating. She'd record what they had to say so their stories could be heard. Because she knew that every day is a gift, that every person matters, even when your story makes other people feel uncomfortable, or you get called names just for being who you are."

Ida felt a wave of relief.

"Aunt Malayka is my hero. Her life ended way too soon. But she's still teaching me how people can look out for one another no matter what we're up against or what pulls us apart, if we listen…and remember."

…Ida noticed that Dad was pacing nervously in the back of the auditorium. But she continued.

"When my teacher gave us this assignment, I had no idea what having a passion in life was. Honestly? I thought my passion was eating ice cream."

Ida waited for some people to stop laughing.

"Now I know my passion is to care about people the way my family does. To work for what's fair—for Palestinians, for our planet, so it can be everybody's home."

From the shadows of the back of the auditorium, Ida saw Dad's arm shoot up in a victory sign as if to say, "Gooooooal!"

Her talk had been short, and there was a silence before the audience realized that she was finished speaking. Then, there was applause.

Some people clapped tentatively. Some people might even have been angry. But Ida felt that at least now they'd heard the truth.

⁕ ⁕

The program ran long and it was past dinnertime, so the fifteen-minute wait for the judges to announce the winner was torturous. Danya and Salwa each held one hand hoping that Ida would win.

Carolina came over and whispered something in Ida's ear, and Ida smiled.

As they waited, Ida caught Danya staring at Carolina's brother, Mario. A second later, Ida couldn't believe it when Mario turned around and smiled at Danya!

"Good taste," Ida whispered to Danya, trying to sound cool.

She was a little scared that Danya would scream at her or insult her as she often did for no apparent reason, but she didn't.

"Oh, Ida, please don't tell Mom. She'll kill me," Danya whispered, both girls knowing that Palestinian girls are not supposed to have boyfriends.

"Of course I won't tell her, silly. I'm your sister."

Danya squeezed her hand to say thank you.

"But..." Ida continued, "If *you* ever decide to tell Mom, I'm absolutely, positively sure she won't be mad."

"You think?" Danya asked hopefully.

"I *know*." Ida said.

⁕ ⁕

The judges, it turned out, couldn't choose one winner so they announced a tie. One first prize winner was Todd Putnam, a boy who had performed an amazing rap song that he wrote himself about the way music can change your life. He had gotten some high school boys to dance, and they had an awesome video in the background.

The other first prize winner was a girl named Angela Gonzalez who had done her presentation about nature. She did a fancy PowerPoint with facts about nature and how people are destroying the earth. She talked with such passion, Ida thought Angela definitely deserved to win.

The two winners each got dinners for their families at a beautiful revolving restaurant that overlooked the river. The big news was that Carolina won an honorable mention for her amazing photographs! After a ton of hugging and hand shaking and a million selfies, Carolina left with her parents and Mario to celebrate at home.

Ida was only a little bit disappointed that she didn't win. Mostly, she was relieved that it was over.

But it wasn't.

Lizzie, Ida's classmate, was walking toward her.

Ida's stomach tightened, expecting some kind of insult.

Lizzie paused, looking unsure if she was welcome. But then she stepped up.

"I liked your presentation," Lizzie said tentatively. "I've been learning about Palestinian refugees. And the right of return."

Ida couldn't believe her ears.

"By the way, I have an old-lady name, too!" Lizzie said, suddenly enthusiastic.

Ida tilted her head, confused.

"Elizabeth?"

Ida laughed out loud, and Lizzie looked relieved.

"Maybe we could get pizza after school sometime?

Just then, Ms. Bloom walked up.

"Effective talk," she said to Ida matter of factly. "You took a risk going the no-tech route, and you relied a lot on your own opinions. But you got your message across."

Just as abruptly, she left.

Ida had never seen Ms. Bloom be so cold. Was it because of something she'd said in her talk?

But Lizzie seemed unfazed. She rolled her eyes and pursed her lips. Ida sensed that Lizzie understood what she was thinking and was on her side.

⋆⁎ ⋆⁎

Ida realized she'd been holding her breath, not just all night, but for weeks or maybe even for years.

She exhaled, and exhaustion washed over her.

"Can we go home now?"

Ida sincerely wanted to be at home, in her own house, in Oldbridge.

"Well..." Mom smiled. "You *are* really good at finding your way home, aren't you, Ida?"

"We thought we'd go out first and eat at that turning restaurant and enjoy the great view of the river," Dad said.

"But I didn't win."

Ida felt for a minute that her father had misunderstood and would feel let down or even ashamed of her.

"You *did* win!" Salwa shouted, a little too loud.

"You're *our* winner," Danya cheered.

"Goooooooal!"

"We could never, ever be ashamed of you, Ida," Dad said as if reading her mind. "We are so, so, so, so, so very proud of you, Ida," Dad said, imitating the way the girls always exaggerated things.

He put his hand solidly on Ida's shoulder so she'd know that he wasn't joking.

"And we have other things to celebrate, too," Dad added, slipping his other arm around Mom's waist, displaying affection they rarely showed in public. He wore a sneaky smile and didn't explain, seeming to want to torture them with their own curiosity.

Then, Mom took the girls' hands in hers and laid them on her stomach.

"It's a boy," she said simply.

A new soccer teammate!—the three sisters jumped around squealing. Even Ida was thrilled.

As they were leaving, Ida looked around for Lizzie. On the other side of the lobby, at almost the same moment, Lizzie had the same idea. They caught one another's attention, and nodded goodbye.

⋆⋆ ☆⋆

Ida and her family enjoyed a delicious meal, and then they strolled along the river in the late spring warmth, sometimes bubbling about funny things that happened during the presentations and sometimes enjoying the silence together. At one point Ida, wanted to ask her family how they thought their lives would be different if they'd never come to the United States, but she decided that it

211

wasn't necessary. Palestine would always be part of them, no matter where they lived.

⋆⁺ ⋆⁺

"*Booza!*" Salwa chirped when she saw a street vendor selling ice cream.

Ida got two scoops of vanilla chocolate chip ice cream, which she ate without a drop of guilt. But she did vow to herself to enjoy her next ice cream sundae in Palestine, with her family…and Layla.

Arabic Terminology

Adhan   The *adhan*, pronounced "a-than," refers to the chant that is broadcast in Arabic from mosques five times a day to let Muslims know that it is time to pray. Timed with the sun, the *adhan* has coordinated daily life in Muslim communities since before clocks were invented.

Allah   *Allah* is the most common Arabic word for God, though *Allah* actually has 99 names. *Allah* is not only referred to in prayer, but is prominent in many common Arabic phrases said throughout the day, by Arabic speakers of all faiths. For example, if you say "*Salamtak*," to wish well-being to a person who is sick, the sick person will respond, "*Allah yisalmak*" which means "may *Allah* protect you."

Askadinya   Small, tart fruit with the texture of an apricot, called loquat in English. "*Askadinya*" literally means "the most delicious in the world." *Askadinya* trees are plentiful in Palestine, but they only give fruit for a short time in early spring.

'Asr
'Asr is the term for the afternoon prayer, the third of the five obligatory daily prayers for Muslims. It can also be a general reference to the afternoon. The apostrophe at the beginning of the word represents the letter *'ayn*, which makes a sound that does not exist in English.

Ayat al-Kursi
There are over 6,000 verses, or *ayah*, in the *Quran*. *Ayat al-Kursi* or "throne verse" is one of the most recited verses. It is often displayed or worn for protection from evil from the devil or supernatural beings called *jinn*.

'Aza
'Aza refers to the three-day mourning period after a death (longer for a widow). It is important for Muslims to show support for the grieving family and also facilitate transition of the person who died to the afterlife, and therefore, attendance at *'azas* is an important social custom.

Basbousa
Basbousa is a sweet, syrup-soaked semolina cake that originated in Egypt, and is also common in other countries, especially during festivals. It is also called *harissa*, although they can be slightly different.

Behar
Depending on the area and the family, *behar* can mean allspice or it can mean a special all-purpose spice blend that may include cardamom, cinnamon, cloves, coriander, cumin, nutmeg, and peppercorns. It is used to season lamb, fish, chicken, beef, and soups.

Arabic Terminology

Booza   *Booza* is the colloquial pronunciation of the word for ice cream. Unlike the heavy cream ice cream that is common in the United States, Arabic ice cream is made with milk instead of cream and eggs, and it gets a unique, stretchy consistency from mastic gum.

Fellaheen   Literally, "farmers" or "peasants," the word *"fellaheen"* refers to Palestinians and other Arabs who live off the land, including all the cultural and social aspects of agriculturally-based communities.

Freekeh   *Freekeh* is wheat harvested while it is green, before it fully ripens. It is similar to bulgur wheat but has a smoky, nutty flavor that develops when it is roasted or smoked, then rubbed to remove the chaff. It can be eaten alongside meat or vegetables or as a soup.

Habibti   Arabic for "my love," (feminine) used for loved ones, not just between lovers. (The masculine term is *habibi*.)

Haj   *Haj* refers to the pilgrimage to Mecca, one of the five pillars of Islam. It is obligatory for able Muslims to complete the *haj* at least once during their lifetime. It is also the term used as a respectful reference to a Muslim man who has completed the pilgrimage. (The female term for "pilgrim" is *hajje*.)

Haram   *Haram* means "forbidden." It refers to behavior that contradicts the teachings of Islam such as killing an innocent person, stealing, eating pork, gambling,

215

drinking alcohol, among other transgressions. In common usage, behavior that is considered bad by tradition may also be called "*haram*."

Hummos   Puréed chickpeas mixed with tahini (sesame paste), lemon juice, garlic and cumin. A common dip eaten with pita bread, it can be a starter salad or sandwich spread.

Ilhamdulilah   Used frequently in conversation to praise God for any outcome, whether good or bad.

Intifada   Literally "shaking off," *intifada* refers to the uprising of Palestinians against Israeli occupation and colonization, especially from 1987-1993 (first *intifada*) and 2000-2005 (second *intifada*).

'Isha   The last of the five daily prayers obligatory for Muslims. It generally occurs about two hours after sundown. Before electricity, Muslims often went to sleep after the *'isha* prayer.

Itfaddal   Can mean "if you please" or "welcome," it is used as an invitation to others.

Jilbab   A long and loose-fitting coat worn over clothes by devout Muslim women. In some communities, the typical *jilbab* is black, but in Palestine they can be of many colors.

Ka'ak   Round or oval tube-shaped rings of bread covered with sesame seeds known as a specialty of Jerusalem. It can be eaten as a snack with salty *za'atar*. Visitors traveling from Jerusalem will often bring Jerusalem *ka'ak* to destinations around Palestine as a treat.

Kaslana   Means lazy (feminine). Like in English, it can be said as an insult or in jest.

Labneh   Slightly salty, thick, milk-based spread. It is made by removing the whey by straining yogurt through cheesecloth for 12-24 hours. It is served, usually for breakfast, drizzled in olive oil.

Lubya   A specific variety of thin green beans stewed in spicy tomato sauce and garnished with lamb or beef. It is often eaten with bread or served over rice.

Maghrib   Meaning "sunset," it refers to the prayer just after sunset, the fourth of the five daily prayers mandated in Islam. It can also be used more generally to refer to the time period just after sunset or to Morocco (because Morocco is to the west of the Middle East, like the sun as it sets).

Marhaba   Arabic greeting meaning "hello." The response would be *marhabteen* or two hellos or *ahlan* or *ahlain*, which mean "welcome."

Maqluba   A traditional one-pot Palestinian casserole that is popular around the Middle East. It is made in layers in a pot on top of the stove. The bottom layer can be fried eggplant or cauliflower, followed by pre-cooked meat or chicken fried in spices. Other layers may include garbanzo beans or other vegetables with rice on the top. After being cooked in spiced broth, the *maqluba* pot is turned over onto a tray, thus earning its name, which means "upside down."

Ma'janaat   Baked goods such as spinach turnovers, small pizzas with ground lamb meat, or biscuits of *za'atar* and cheese. They can be served as a snack or light meal.

Molokhiyya   A very commonly available leafy green vegetable called Jew's Mallow in English that is chopped finely and cooked with or without meat into a stew or soup with a slimy texture. It is a favorite of Palestinian children, and also extremely healthy.

Mukhaddir   In the old days, the *mukhaddir* was the villager hired to guard the village fields from theft or damage. The *mukhaddir* made sure that herders didn't graze their livestock on the cultivated land of other villagers. The *mukhaddir* role faded out of practice around the 1960s.

Nakba   Used by Palestinians to refer to the loss of Palestine upon the establishment of the State of Israel in 1948, often translated as "the catastrophe." Many refer to the continued violence of exile, occupation and colonization as the "ongoing *Nakba*."

Quran   The *Quran* is Islam's holy book. It is believed by Muslims to be the literal word of God, orally revealed to the final prophet, Muhammad, over a period of some 23 years, beginning in the month of Ramadan. It was scribed by several of the prophet's companions as the Prophet Muhammad could not write. The *Quran* is considered the culmination of a series of divine messages starting with those revealed to Adam, including the Torah, the Psalms and the Gospel.

Sabaya   Young women

Shabab   Young men or a mixed-gender group of youth.

Shekel   The currency of the State of Israel, also used by Palestinians in all areas that Israel controls. Some Palestinian transactions also take place in Jordanian dinars, US dollars or euros.

Shukran   "Thank you." One common response is *afwan*.

Siddo   Affectionate term for grandfather in Arabic.

Sitti   Affectionate term for grandmother in Arabic.

Sura   A chapter of the *Quran*, comprised of verses (*ayaat*).

Wad or wadi   Dry riverbed

Za'atar   A staple in Palestinian diets, *za'atar* is a dried herb blend made from wild thyme and sesame seeds, eaten with bread and olive oil. Israel declared wild thyme protected and therefore illegal to pick, which Palestinians consider discriminatory.

Gratitude

My deepest appreciation to the Palestinian people—to the old man in the grocery store who sold me phone cards, to my upstairs neighbor whose tea was sweet, to the grumpy bus drivers who took me across checkpoints, and to the women who taught me to cook the food my kids love. I have always felt welcome as a member of their community, even though I am not Palestinian. And over the years, I have been honored to stand with them in their struggle for liberation.

But although I have spent more than half my life navigating Palestine as an "insider-outsider" and mothering my beloved Palestinian-American daughters, I am still learning. Like Ida, my journey is not merely from one place to another, but from one "me" to an ever-expanding realization of myself. I hope that my growth—and Ida's—inspires readers to connect with their own varied and complex identities, and with Palestinians.

★ ☆★

My daughters—Serene, Jassi and Maysanne—used to walk in a line like ducks into Doctor Maha's pediatric office in Sheikh Jarrah, Jerusalem. They pulled thick paperbacks from their backpacks and stuck their noses in, much to the astonishment of the tired parents and sniffling children who filled the bustling waiting room. My girls' voracious reading made me jealous of the writers who knew how to captivate, so I decided to try to learn.

I think reading helps fill the achy spaces in my girls' binational, bicultural, bilingual lives, and writing helps me to fill my own achy spaces as a Jew who knows things that are painful to know.

Mothering my Palestinian-American daughters gave this book a purpose, to make visible the despair and the potential, the doubt and the humor that whirl about in a family with Palestine at its center. Raising my daughters in the West Bank, where this book was written, provided the dusty colors and earthy smells of Ida's story.

In addition to providing inspiration, my daughters' brilliant editorial, artistic and logistical support were invaluable at every step. Maysanne deserves a special shout-out for her tireless and loving hand holding during uphill patches.

My husband, Hani, who is *not* a passionate reader of fiction, was a major contributor nonetheless. I would say that his knowledge of Palestinian history and culture is encyclopedic, but that would be backwards. It is the keepers of oral history, like Hani, who safeguard knowledge and gift it to the next generation and to non-Palestinian learners like me. Many of Hani's razor-sharp memories spring from his early childhood, serving cola to the neighborhood farmers as they sat together at the end of a hot day. They offer a soon-to-be-closed window into how challenges were faced by his parents, grandparents and their grandparents and into their hopes. Every page of this book is informed by the truth that was born into his bones, and my own deep respect for my treasured family-in-law, their hard work and their integrity.

Abdelfattah AbuSrour, Micha Kurz and Abu Fu'ad and the staff, teachers and students of the Riyad Al-Aksa School in Jerusalem's Old City explained things I couldn't otherwise have understood.

Gratitude

My special thanks to my champions: Lucy O'Brien, David Hales, Rima Hassouneh, Abeer Ramadan-Shinnawi, Abigail Abysalh-Metzger, Vicki Tamoush, and so many others who read drafts, offered ideas, advice, and encouragement or made connections; and thanks-plus-hugs to Shaima Farouki and Nabila El Haitout for invaluable help with cover concepts.

I am infinitely grateful to my beta readers, adult and kid alike, who gave feedback that improved the book tremendously, including Lilian Calley, Nishan Ghanayem, Evan Hare, Mary Neznek, Joan Litman, and my mother, Katharine Sharfman Lester.

And where would I be without book lovers—readers, teachers, librarians, booksellers, and so many defenders of literature? In that effort, Interlink stands out among publishers for their commitment to bringing Palestinian themes to readers, regardless of pushback from forces that would deny Palestinian humanity. To Michel Moushabeck, publisher, Maha Moushabeck, Harrison Williams, Pamela Fontes-May, Sadie Trombetta, Brenda Eaton and to the entire staff at Interlink, my heartfelt thanks.

Lastly, my gratitude to John Sobhieh Fiscella at Interlink, one of the many unsung editors who midwife books that change our lives. John got deep into the weeds of the story, the setting, the characters' dreams and their imperfections. As a result of John's high standards and genuine caring, this book is much better than it would have been without his stewardship, and I am a better writer. John *understands* storytelling. There are no words to describe how fortunate I am to have him on my team.

✦ ✦

An educator's guide for this book, and a wealth of other resources for teaching and learning about Palestine, can be found at *www.IdaInTheMiddle.com*.

Other Interlink Books by Nora Lester Murad

I Found Myself in Palestine: Stories of Love and Renewal from around the Globe

Rest in My Shade: A Poem About Roots

More information is available at www.noralestermurad.com